Chapter One: Drowning in Silence

Callie gripped the edge of the nurse's station, her hands trembling—not from fatigue, but from the weight of another day that demanded too much and gave back nothing.

Five patients. Two admits. One fresh from surgery. A med pass that never stopped. Alarms buzzed like a twisted lullaby, and somewhere down the hall, a monitor chirped a rhythm she couldn't unhear. There was no pause. Just movement. Just survival.

"Callie," came the soft voice of the charge nurse, "you've got another admit."

The words landed like bricks. Her jaw clenched. She didn't answer, didn't nod. Just stared at the dry-erase board on the wall like it might blink back in solidarity. Instead, it mocked her—color-coded priorities, checkboxes for hourly rounding, smiley faces meant to prove they were "engaged in patient care."

A fucking whiteboard. That's what mattered.

Not that Mrs. Thompson hadn't had her pain meds in over an hour. Not that Callie hadn't eaten since a granola bar at 6 a.m. Not that her youngest had cried when she left that morning and she'd pretended not to hear it.

But that board? If it wasn't updated, she could expect a clipboard audit from management with all the grace of a guillotine.

She glanced at the hallway—family members hovered like ghosts, staff moved like automatons. Her smile didn't reach her eyes anymore, and her laugh was a script she no longer believed in.

She wanted to scream.

To say no.

To tear the whole goddamn system down and make them see what it cost just to keep breathing in this place.

But instead, she reached for her med scanner.

The unit buzzed with barely-contained chaos. Callie moved between rooms, adjusting pumps, checking vitals, smoothing sheets like she could press away the cracks in the system one corner at a time.

At the med room, she caught sight of herself in the cabinet glass—mask hanging under her chin, eyes ringed with exhaustion, hair frizzing from the humidity of effort. Her badge said *RN*, but some days it felt more like *sacrificial offering*. She looked like hell. And for a moment, she didn't want to fix it.

Tasha, another nurse, passed her with a telemetry machine in one hand and a coffee she hadn't sipped in hours.

"You good?" she asked.

"Living the dream," Callie said flatly.

Tasha snorted. "If this is the dream, I hope I wake up soon."

Callie smirked, but the humor didn't settle. Not anymore. It used to be enough—jokes, memes, sarcastic vents in the breakroom. But now it just echoed. Hollow.

Back at the nurse's station, the dry-erase board glared from the wall, pristine and meaningless. She'd updated it. That's what mattered. Not the short staffing. Not the unsafe ratios. Not the twenty-minute delay in getting morphine to a post-op patient because pharmacy was short too.

But God forbid a whiteboard go untouched. Whiteboards saved lives. Or at least, that's what the clipboard cult believed.

She remembered the last time there'd been a charting error. Instead of addressing the chaos—the broken printer, the float nurse with eight patients, the call lights that never stopped—leadership handed her a worksheet. A real piece of paper that basically asked:

"How did you screw this up?"

The answer was simple.

She hadn't.

The system had.

By the end of the shift, the halls were quieter. Not because things had calmed—but because everyone had shut down.

Callie walked past the crash cart someone had half-heartedly restocked. Past the fresh urine spill no one had time to clean. Past the float nurse crying silently in the breakroom because she'd just made her first med error.

She slid into Room 420, checked vitals, changed a dressing, adjusted pillows. Her patient—paraplegic, sharp-witted, and kind—smiled at her with soft eyes.

"You're my favorite nurse," the woman said simply.

Callie blinked. Smiled. Said thank you. And suddenly hated herself for how much that one sentence undid her. She wasn't trying to be anyone's favorite. She was just trying to survive the shift without breaking. And today, that compliment felt like a taunt. A reminder that she still cared enough to be crushed by kindness.

The patient's mother nodded from the window. "She said that when we first got here. That you actually *see* her."

Callie didn't cry. She never cried at work. But her throat burned like hell.

Instead, she smirked, tilting her head just enough to let the sass back in. "Well, I accept bribes. Chocolate, iced coffee, or cash. Hospital policy."

The room laughed. For a moment, the weight lifted. But as she left, the heaviness returned. The gratitude felt too sharp. Like being thanked for holding back a flood with bare hands.

The parking garage was nearly empty when she finally clocked out. One flickering light overhead. The kind that makes you feel like even the universe is short-staffed.

She slid into her dented SUV, threw her badge onto the passenger seat, and gripped the steering wheel until her knuckles ached.

Then the tears came.

Not a breakdown. Not even a sob.

Just quiet, hot tears—silent but violent, like everything inside her decided to quit without notice.

"Living the dream," she muttered to the dashboard. "Well... someone's dream."

She started the car. The Bluetooth picked up mid-song—some overly cheerful pop track that clashed violently with the storm inside her chest.

She didn't change it. Just let it play. Like a soundtrack to her unraveling, cheerful and mocking.

On the drive home, she talked to herself.

Not out loud. Not yet. Just thoughts bouncing like debris in her mind.

> "I updated the whiteboard. That's all that matters, right?"

> "Mrs. Hennessy was hypotensive, but her name was written in purple marker, so we're good."

> "They'll give me another self-audit next week. Ask how I could've 'prevented' the error I didn't have time to catch."

Her grip tightened on the steering wheel.

> "I can't keep doing this."

She said it out loud that time. The words sat heavy in the air. Real.

"Let them come for me. Let them hand me another clipboard and tell me it's 'growth.' I'll light the whole damn thing on fire."

And somewhere in the silence that followed—beneath the sarcasm, beneath the guilt, beneath the survival-mode routine that had become her entire life—a spark caught.

It didn't flare. Not yet.

But it burned. Quiet. Dangerous. Persistent.

She didn't know it yet, but that drive home was the beginning.

Not of healing.

Not of rest.

But of fire.

Of change. Of a woman finally done surviving a system built to break her.

Chapter Two: Static and Sparks

Callie dropped her bag by the front door and kicked off her shoes—one landing near the coat rack, the other disappearing into the chaos of scattered sneakers, LEGO landmines, and a sticky juice box someone left half-drunk on the entryway table.

The house smelled faintly of spaghetti, and something vaguely burnt. She took a breath. At least they'd eaten.

Before she could step further, the thundering stampede arrived—three boys launching toward her like she was the finish line in a race only they had the energy for.

"Mom!"
 "Mommy!"
 "Guess what happened!"

Sticky fingers latched onto her scrub top. One had chocolate smeared on his face. Another was barefoot. The third clutched a science fair flyer like it was a golden ticket.

Callie braced herself against the wall, her body barely keeping up. Her voice came out hoarse from twelve hours of talking over alarms and pretending she was fine.

"Go easy. I'm held together by coffee, spite, and a dream I forgot to keep dreaming."

They laughed. She smiled. Real, this time. It hurt her cheeks.

Her mom popped her head out of the kitchen. "They're bathed, fed, and mostly homeworked. Left you a plate in the microwave. Don't ask what it is. Just trust me."

Callie gave her a look that was half gratitude, half guilt. "You're a saint."

Her mom shrugged. "I'm retired. This is the easy shift."

Callie wasn't sure if that was true, but she didn't argue. She crouched low and pulled her youngest into her arms, ignoring the ache in her back and the wet spot forming on her shoulder from someone's fruit punch mouth. She inhaled the top of his head like it was oxygen. Maybe it was.

"Okay, let's take it down a notch," she murmured, voice softening. "Mom needs to sit down before she faceplants."

The boys dispersed in a blur of shouts and toy negotiations. Callie sank onto the couch, her legs throbbing, her brain still moving at hospital speed.

Later, with the boys tucked into their beds and her mom folding laundry in the other room, Callie sat at the kitchen table, her microwaved dinner going cold. Again.

She didn't need to reheat it. The heat would come from her chest in waves anyway—rage disguised as fatigue.

Her mom poured two mugs of tea and joined her, settling in like a woman who had survived things no one ever documented.

"Tough shift?"

Callie didn't answer right away. She stared at her food like she might absorb nutrients just by proximity.

Finally: "A woman coded and no one knew because we were drowning. A patient told me I was her favorite and it made me want to cry. I laughed about whiteboards while my soul disintegrated. And I cried in my car. Again."

Her mom blew on her tea. "So a normal day, then."

Callie gave a crooked smile, dry and tired. "Guess I missed the part where trauma came standard in the onboarding packet."

Her mom didn't flinch. Just sipped her tea like it was armor. "As long as you still have your humor, you'll make it."

Callie didn't respond right away. Didn't laugh either. Just stared at the mug in her hand like it might start leaking. "Yeah," she finally said. "But what if that's the first thing to go?"

They sat in silence for a beat, the kind that happens when someone knows your life too well to offer platitudes.

"I don't get it," Callie said finally. "How did we get here? How did the work become the easy part, and everything around it the hell?"

Her mom leaned back, eyes tired but clear. "When I started, we kept our heads down, did our work, and hoped we didn't kill anybody. That was enough. The system was never built for sustainability. Just survival."

"Survival's just the prelude to burnout. I want more than not dying." Callie muttered. "I'm tired of patching holes in a sinking ship and being told to smile while we drown."

Her mom studied her face. "I remember that feeling."

Callie raised an eyebrow. "You do?"

"Of course. The first time I realized we were numbers, not nurses. The first time I watched a patient suffer because the supply room was locked and the key was missing and no one gave a damn." She stirred her tea. "They didn't blacklist you. They just ghosted you until you disappeared yourself."

Callie's jaw tightened. "Then maybe that's the problem. We've been quiet too long."

Her mom gave her a long look. "Fighting takes more than anger. It takes endurance. Timing. Allies."

Callie blinked. "So what, wait for permission?"

"No." Her voice was firm. "But choose your moment. Burnout isn't a battle plan. It's a warning."

They fell silent again. This time, it wasn't heavy. Just true.

Later, after her mom had gone to bed and the house fell into that rare, sacred stillness—no call lights, no alarms, no policy updates in all-caps emails—Callie curled up on the couch with her phone.

She unlocked her phone, thumb hovering. Memes. Mantras. Mental breakdowns set to trending audio. Coping, rebranded. Just enough to make surviving feel like an aesthetic.

She opened the nurse group chat out of habit. Someone had shared a meme of a nurse crying in a med room. She tapped open the post, the comments scrolling fast:

"Same girl. I can't do this much longer."
"It's the ratios for me."
"Anyone else starting to feel… done?"

She stared at the screen.

She wanted to say something. Wanted to throw a match into the center of that grief and see who would stand beside her.

Instead, she typed something small. Quiet.

> Anyone else notice how we never get asked before policies change? Just handed more and told it's 'best practice'?

She hovered. Thumb paused.

Then: **send**.

If silence was complicity, maybe this was her first act of treason.

No emoji. No exclamation mark. Just a whisper into the static.

She sat back, phone still in her hand, heart thudding— not from fear. From *feeling*. From being awake again.

The house creaked. A pipe groaned in the wall. Outside, the wind stirred against the windows.

Inside, something stirred in her too.

Not loud. Not yet.

But undeniable.

She checked on the boys before bed. Her youngest had curled into a ball, his foot hanging off the side of the mattress. The middle one clutched his worn shark plush with a death grip. Her oldest—her thinker—had kicked off the covers again and mumbled in his sleep.

She sat at the edge of his bed for a moment too long, brushing his hair back from his forehead.

He stirred.

"Mom?"

"I'm here, baby."

He blinked, eyes bleary but aware. "Will you be home tomorrow night?"

Her heart clenched. Not "Can we play?" Not "Can we watch a movie?"

Just *will you be home.*

"Maybe," she said softly. "I hope so."

He nodded like he understood too well, then rolled over.

Callie swallowed the ache and backed out of the room.

That question should've wrecked her. Instead, it just joined the pile of things she'd already stopped reacting to.

In her bedroom, she didn't even turn on the light. She sat on the edge of the bed, still in her scrubs, and stared at the floor.

The overtime was supposed to get them to Disney. That was the dream. One week of magic. One week where she could say *yes* to everything. One week where the guilt could take a vacation too.

She pulled out her planner. A crumpled Disney flyer peeked from the back pocket.

Next to it was the policy update she'd printed two shifts ago—the one that quietly shoved IV start responsibilities back onto floor nurses without training, input, or warning.

Callie stared at both papers for a long moment.

Dream. Reality.

Fantasy. Burnout.

She didn't cry. She didn't rage.

She felt everything. And nothing. Like grief in slow motion.

The system didn't need to kill her. It just needed her to keep showing up.

And beneath it all—under the numbness, under the exhaustion, under the constant juggling of lives and policies and kids—there was a flicker.

Not hope.

Not yet.

But awareness.

And the beginning of a voice that wouldn't stay silent forever.

Chapter Three: The Cracks Beneath the Surface

The air was thick with bleach and burnout.

Callie stepped off the elevator onto the swing floor—where the hospital sent its leftovers. Overflow, post-ops, confused elderly, GI bleeds, stepdowns no one had room for. A little of everything, and not enough of anything.

It was 6:47 a.m., and the floor already buzzed like an overworked heart—seconds from arrest.

She pulled her badge, clocked in, and grabbed her assignment sheet from the whiteboard. Seven names. One patient on a PCA pump. Two with mobility issues. One fresh from the ER who hadn't been medicated since admission. And no tech. Again.

She rubbed her eyes. "Oh good. Another episode of 'Survivor: Healthcare," she muttered under her breath.

The charge nurse—Dana, already frazzled—barely looked up.

"404's a fall risk," Dana said, scribbling on a form. "They tried to get out of bed twice last night."

Callie nodded, scanning her group. IV antibiotics, wound care, an NPO stroke patient with no updated orders, and someone needing frequent glucose checks on a sliding scale that looked more like a math problem than a care plan.

She stopped asking for help. The silence answered quicker.

By 8:00 a.m., Callie had already been paged for 406's insulin, cleaned up 407's accident, and sent pharmacy a reminder for the Levaquin that still hadn't arrived.

The insulin pen wasn't labeled. New tech.

"Check the fridge," Callie said gently. "If it's not in the bin with their name, don't guess. This patient's renal—we can't risk a drop."

The tech looked grateful and overwhelmed. "Thanks."

Callie nodded, already halfway to the next room. She wanted to tell him to *run*. Before he got good enough to stop crying and start dissociating.

The day was just beginning, and she was already twenty minutes behind.

At 9:17, a call light blinked red.

Room 410. Emergency assistance requested.

Callie dropped her scanner and ran. Her heart hit her ribs like a code bell. Adrenaline didn't ask for permission anymore—it just showed up and took over.

Inside, her patient—an elderly woman two days post-hip repair—was halfway out of bed, tangled in the side rails. Her legs shook under her. She was pale, breath ragged, eyes wide with panic.

Callie reached her fast, one hand on the patient's shoulder, the other fumbling for the bed controls.

"You're okay," she said. "Let's get you back down."

The CNA, Lucy, appeared in the doorway, wide-eyed.

"Call for the lift," Callie ordered. "Grab vitals. Don't pull the IV."

Lucy hesitated, frozen.

There wasn't time to freeze. Not when lives could bleed out in seconds.

Callie looked her in the eye. "Now."

Lucy blinked, nodded, and rushed out.

She didn't have time to soothe. Just delegate or drown.

They got the patient back into bed without injury, but Callie's heart was pounding as she documented the fall risk escalation. The patient's chart had no updated sitter order. The hourly rounding log, already incomplete, would flag the incident.

She knew what leadership would see: a missed box.

Not the four other patients she was caring for. Not the shortage. Not the system.

Just the unchecked box.

The fall risk wouldn't be the problem. The incomplete checkbox would.

By mid-morning huddle, Callie had given up on coffee. She leaned against the wall with her arms folded, listening as the nurse educator passed around a quote card laminated in bright pastel.

"'Success is the sum of small efforts repeated day in and day out,'" the educator chirped.

Callie muttered, "So is trauma," and turned back to her assignment.

Someone should laminate one that says, 'Congrats on surviving another preventable disaster.'

The huddle ended with an email reminder: new IV policy coming soon. Details TBD.

Great. That never meant more support. It meant more work.

Back on the floor, the vibe was off.

The supply room was missing half the wound care kits. The bladder scanner was MIA—again. And someone had unplugged the crash cart to plug in their phone.

Callie re-taped the plug, flagged it for Biomed, and silently begged the universe to give them one quiet shift.

Instead, she passed Marla from ortho—seasoned, sharp, usually unshakable—standing in the med room with her eyes closed and her hand pressed to the cabinet.

She wasn't praying. She was bargaining. 'Just one shift without a sentinel event. Just one.'

Callie didn't interrupt. Just kept walking, her stomach sinking.

At 11:52 a.m., Callie was checking blood sugars when she heard arguing near the nurses' station.

A travel nurse was on the phone with pharmacy.

"I told the resident that order was off-label. Now they're blaming me for the delay?"

She slammed the receiver down, her face flushed.

Callie handed her a spare alcohol swab.

It wasn't support. It was a truce—between women holding the line with duct tape and caffeine.

It wasn't much.

But it was something.

Just after noon, Callie stepped into Room 405, a quiet post-op patient resting under warm blankets. He looked up as she adjusted his IV tubing.

"You're the first person who looked me in the eye today," he said.

Callie paused.

His voice wasn't bitter. Just lonely.

"Thank you," he added. "For seeing me."

Callie blinked fast.

She smiled. "Don't go spoiling me now. I'm already working overtime."

He laughed softly, and she adjusted his pillow with a little more care.

She didn't let herself feel it—too dangerous.

But it got in anyway.

In the breakroom, Callie dropped into the far corner with a protein bar she couldn't taste. The microwave buzzed as someone reheated soup for the third time. No one spoke.

Her phone buzzed. A message from her oldest:

> "When you're done saving people, can you help me with math?"
> "It's okay if not. I know you're tired."

Her throat tightened.

He didn't mean it to hurt. But it did.

Across the room, Jules walked in, her hair in a frizzed-out bun, badge clipped sideways.

"They updated the IV policy," Jules said, dropping into the chair across from her. "Peripheral starts are ours now. Doesn't matter if the patient's on blood thinners, scared of needles, or if we've got three admits at once."

Callie raised an eyebrow. "No consults at all?"

Jules nodded. "Nope. But the email had emojis, so it's fine."

Callie snorted. "Did they laminate the bullshit too, or just email it?"

"They'll probably print it on cupcakes next week."

Callie leaned her head back against the wall.

Her arms were buzzing. Not from fatigue.

From *rage*.

But she didn't move.

Didn't speak.

Jules cracked open a granola bar. "You okay?"

Callie shook her head. "I keep thinking… maybe the real goal is to break us just enough that we stop asking why."

Jules didn't argue.

The silence between them felt sharp. Familiar. Full of things that couldn't be said in emails or meetings.

Callie looked down at her phone again. Her son's text sat there, blinking.

She couldn't fix pharmacy.

She couldn't rewrite policies.

She couldn't be everywhere at once.

But maybe—just maybe—she could answer this one.

She tapped out a reply with trembling fingers:

>*"Of course. I'll call you before dinner."*

She hit send and exhaled.

The breakroom buzzed with the soft hum of the vending machine and the scraping of chairs.

Outside, the hospital moved on. Alarms. Overhead calls. The shuffle of sneakers on linoleum.

Inside, something shifted.

Not loud.

Not revolutionary.

Just a quiet resistance.

A refusal to disappear.

Because the system didn't care.

But maybe the nurses still could.

Chapter Four: The Breaking Point

The unit was too quiet.

Not in a peaceful way. In the way that made Callie's skin crawl.

Alarms still buzzed. Phones still rang. The overhead intercom still spat out names like bingo numbers. But something about the air felt... off. Like the building was holding its breath.

She scanned the assignment sheet as the charge nurse handed it off with a shrug.

"They floated you from the swing floor to med-surg again. Sorry. We're short."

They were always short.

Callie didn't argue. She'd stopped expecting apologies to come with solutions.

Seven patients. One a fresh ER admit. Two bed alarms. One trach. A post-op on a pain pump. And Dorothy Hennessy—quiet, frail, stable. Still pending DNR paperwork. Still waiting on a physician who was "rounding soon."

The chart said Dorothy had mild dementia and a touch of CHF. What it didn't say was that she smiled when you adjusted her pillows and called everyone sweetheart without irony.

Callie made a mental note to check in on her between med passes. "Between," of course, being theoretical.

The shift hit hard from the start.

At 08:42, Room 216's blood pressure plummeted. Post-op bleed.

The new grad—green, kind, and two heartbeats away from panic—stared at the transfusion order like it was in another language.

"I've never done one," she whispered. "I—I don't want to screw it up."

Callie glanced at the clock. She still hadn't rounded on half her group. But a patient with a ruptured vessel didn't have time for fear.

"I've got it," she said, already pulling the tubing.

She walked her through the process—label check, tubing prime, double verify. The patient was pale, confused. Sweating through the gown. By the time the first bag started dripping, Callie's hands were shaking.

Not from adrenaline.

From rage.

She shouldn't have been the only one who could handle this. But the nurse, who normally precepted new nurses on transfusions, had called out sick. No backup. No IV team. Just whoever was still standing.

She charted in bursts between helping stabilize the patient. Vitals every fifteen. No response from pharmacy on a held med. The CNA assigned to Dorothy's hallway had paged twice. There was no record of a reply.

Callie didn't even know yet.

The overhead speaker crackled.

"Code Blue, Room 219. Code Blue, Room 219."

Callie froze. Her stomach dropped.

Dorothy.

She sprinted.

Room 219 was a storm.

A nurse was doing compressions. Respiratory was fumbling with the airway drawer, which stuck halfway open before jamming. The crash cart's charge light was off. No one had checked it.

Dorothy lay still, skin gray-blue around the lips. Her gown was damp with sweat, IV tubing slack. Her monitor blinked a soft red warning—too little, too late.

Callie shoved gloves on, tried to find a pulse, already knowing.

There was none.

"Anyone know last contact?" someone asked.

No one answered.

The CNA who had paged stood frozen in the doorway, eyes glassy. "I called for help," she said. "Twice. No one came."

No one had time.

They worked on Dorothy for twenty minutes.

It didn't matter.

She was already gone.

Later, Callie sat in the supply room, a warm saline flush still clutched in her hand. She hadn't meant to grab it. Just muscle memory.

Her badge lanyard twisted between her fingers, tight enough to bite into her palm.

Jules found her there. Didn't knock. Didn't say much. Just leaned against the wall and slid to the floor beside her.

They sat in silence.

Finally, Callie spoke. Her voice was low. Raw.

"She paged. The tech. She tried to tell us."

Jules nodded.

"She didn't die because someone missed a check," Callie said, staring at the floor. "She died because no one had the time to care."

Callie's phone buzzed in her scrub pocket.

> *"Mom, are you still helping with math tonight?"*
> *"It's okay if not. Just let me know."*

Her chest tightened.
 She had said yes. She'd meant it.
 But Dorothy died. And Callie never called.

The drive home was silent. Her music didn't auto-connect. She didn't fix it.

Her mom had already put the boys to bed. The dishes were washed. The science flyer still sat on the table.

She stood in the hallway for a long time, unsure what to say.

To anyone.

To herself.

Jules had said, *She's not the first.*

Callie knew that.

But maybe—just maybe—she was the last straw.

This didn't happen because someone missed a check.
It happened because no one had time to check.

Chapter Five: Fallout

Callie sat stiff in the metal chair across from Risk Management.

The room was too bright. The air was too cold. Like a freezer made to preserve blame.

She hadn't even had time to change out of her scrubs. A faint smear of dried blood still stained her sleeve—a ghost from the transfusion earlier.

They said it was a "clinical review."

She knew better.

Across the table sat three people in suits and calm, polite expressions. They reviewed the case file like it was a sandwich order. Not a death. Not a woman who'd called her "sweetheart" and smiled every time you fixed her blanket.

Angela shuffled papers. That was her role, apparently.

"Let's begin the review of the Hennessy incident," she said. "Time of deterioration: approximately 16:42. No response to stimuli recorded at 17:06. Code called at 17:09."

Callie clenched her jaw. She didn't need a timeline— she'd lived it.

"I was in 216," she said evenly. "The new grad was initiating a blood transfusion. She didn't know how. Mr. Alvarez was crashing."

Angela didn't look up. "According to documentation, the tech noted altered mentation around 16:30, but there was no nursing reassessment prior to code activation."

Callie blinked. "There was no one else. Jules was in 328 with a behavioral. Linda was on the phone with pharmacy over a med order the resident screwed up. We had one tech. No secretary. You want me to clone myself?"

Angela cleared her throat. "We're just trying to identify where process improvement is needed."

"Oh, screw your processes," Callie snapped, her voice shaking. "I kept someone else alive. You want me to apologize for that?"

Silence.

Even Jules didn't breathe too loud.

Angela finally looked up. "We just want to ensure this doesn't happen again."

"It will happen again," Callie said. "Because nothing's changed. Dorothy didn't die because we missed a round. She died because the whole floor runs on fumes, and you all pretend that's sustainable."

Her fingernails dug into her palms. She thought of the monitor blinking red. The uncharged crash cart. The ignored page.

"There seems to be some discrepancy in the rapid response timeline," someone else added carefully. "Can you walk us through your decision to delay—"

"I didn't delay," Callie said flatly. "I saved a life."

Jules, two chairs over, shifted forward.

"She's not wrong," she said calmly. "Callie was doing a transfusion because I asked her to. The new grad froze. I couldn't get there in time. Dorothy wasn't ignored—she was unreachable."

Angela opened her mouth. Closed it.

"We're not asking for perfection," another administrator said carefully. "Just accountability."

Jules smiled without humor. "Then start at the top."

Callie sat back. Her breath was shaky, but her spine was straight.

They would document. They would deflect.

But she was done pretending this was okay.

Back on the floor, things moved like nothing had happened.

Alarms. Lunch trays. Call lights.

Mr. Caldwell, half-lucid and fully inappropriate, shouted from Room 17.

"Hey baby, shake that ass for me!"

Callie didn't flinch. "Keep your hands to yourself, Mr. Caldwell, or you're losing your pudding privileges."

He grumbled. She kept walking.

Down the hall, a patient lashed out at a CNA. A tray crashed. Someone yelled for security.

Callie moved faster than she should have.

"Lucy, you okay?" she asked, blocking the patient's reach with her own body.

The CNA nodded, shaken.

Callie steadied the situation. Gloved hands. Calm voice.

Her chest was tight.

Not from panic. Not from fear.

From *something else.*

Something heavier.

She glanced at the clock. Ten more hours.

She could do this.

She had to.

But this time—it didn't feel like survival.

This time, it felt like momentum.

Something had shifted.

Something was coming.

Chapter Six: Rumors in the Vents

Callie heard it before she saw it: the shift in the hallway noise.

Not louder, just... sharper. Conversations dipped when she passed. Side glances. The kind that weren't curious—they were calculating.

She clocked in and grabbed her assignment without a word.

Six patients. One fresh transfer from ICU. No tech. No secretary. Again.

"Callie," the charge nurse said, not quite meeting her eyes, "can you take 217? The admit's technically surgical, but they're dumping him here."

Callie nodded. No protest. No sigh. She'd learned there was no point.

But she saw it.

The tension in the nurse's shoulders.

The fear.

Because Callie had become radioactive.

She wasn't "team player Callie" anymore. She was the nurse who'd been in a Risk Management review. The one who told the truth in a room full of people paid to pretend otherwise.

And in a system this fragile, *truth was a threat*.

She checked on 217, updated vitals, charted in bursts. By mid-morning, whispers were swirling in the breakroom.

"You didn't hear it from me—"

"They're watching badges now."
"I heard Dorothy's family filed something."

A nurse leaned in, voice low. "They're saying a tech ignored her vitals for an hour. That's the story admin's pushing."

Callie froze. "That's not what happened."

The nurse looked away. "I know. But they need someone to blame."

In the staff restroom, someone had taped up a ripped piece of notebook paper.

The handwriting was sharp. Controlled.

We know Dorothy wasn't the first.
How many more before they listen?

Callie stared at it for a long moment.

No signature. No logo. Just ink and pressure.

The paper was gone by the end of the shift.

That night, Callie sat on the couch, her legs tucked beneath her. Her youngest had passed out in the middle of the living room, one sock on, sticky fingers curled around a juice box.

Her oldest was at the table, math book open, pencil tapping.

"Want help?" she asked, voice tentative.

He looked up, surprised. Then shrugged. "Sure. If you want."

She sat beside him, heart already twisting.

They worked through fractions—Callie's brain barely cooperating—but they laughed twice. Once when she confused a denominator with a dosage. Again when he corrected her.

"Mom," he said later, "you're better at people than numbers."

She smiled, kissed the top of his head. "Good thing I picked the right profession, then."

But she wasn't sure that was true anymore.

Her mom sat across from her after the kids were down.

"You're quieter than usual," she said.

Callie sipped her tea. "I'm just… watching."

"Watching what?"

"Everyone."

Her mom didn't ask more. She didn't need to.

The next day, in a corner of the breakroom where cell service usually lagged, Callie's phone buzzed with a new message.

**From: Unknown
Display Name: Florence_Nightingale.Burnbook**

> *We've been tracking ratios, near misses, response times. Anonymously. Encrypted.*
> *You're not alone.*
> *Just… don't stop asking questions.*

She stared at the message.

Then another ping.

A second nurse. This one real name, real badge.

> *Heard what you said in the review.*
> *Took guts.*
> *About damn time someone said it out loud.*

That afternoon, a CNA handed her a folded piece of paper. No note. Just handed it over like it was a hallway pass.

Inside:

> *There are more of us than you think.*
> *They count on us staying quiet.*

In the hallway outside Room 220, a nurse from nights passed her and whispered:
 "You didn't screw up. You spoke up. There's a difference."

Back in the breakroom, end of shift, the room was empty but for a vending machine that still refused to take coins.

Callie sat alone.

She opened her phone.

Typed a message into the nurse group:

> *"What if we stop waiting for change and start being it?"*

Her thumb hovered.

She could feel the fear. The weight of it.

She deleted it.

Typed it again.

Added:

> *No more silence. No more blame without a voice. No more watching each other break alone.*

SEND

She tucked her phone into her pocket, leaned back, and exhaled.

Outside the breakroom, nothing had changed.

Not yet.

But in the vents—in the whispers, the notes, the messages—something was building.

And this time, Callie wasn't the only one holding the match.

———————————

Chapter 6.5 – The First Code

The room was too bright.

That's the first thing Callie remembered.

Not the alarms.

Not the voice over the intercom.

Just that unnatural, buzzing-white light overhead—the kind that made everything feel sterile and wrong.

She was three weeks into orientation.

Her badge still said STUDENT.

Her confidence hadn't even made it out of the packaging yet.

She was charting blood sugars when it hit.

Code Blue. Room 412.

Right across the hall.

She'd seen it in simulations.

Plastic dummies. Clean lines. Soft-voiced instructors.

But real codes don't sound like CPR class.

They sound like panic disguised as protocol.

They sound like someone yelling "Charge to 200!" while another voice whispers "Who the hell gave insulin before labs?"

They sound like the nurse next to you saying "Move— just get out of the way" when your hands are shaking too hard to rip the ambu bag from the wall.

They didn't save him.

Callie didn't know his name.

No one said it.

Just "the diabetic in 412."

And after?

They wiped the bed down, reset the tray table, and asked who could take the admit coming up in an hour.

She slipped into the med room and stared at the shelves of syringes and saline flushes like they might offer an explanation.

Her chest was tight.

Hands still trembling.

Vision blurry—not from tears.

From shock.

The kind that sinks in when you realize you didn't save a life. You just stood there and watched it end.

She didn't cry until the charge nurse walked in and said:

Callie nodded.

Lied.

And added:

The charge paused.

Didn't soften.

Just said:

Callie swore, right then, that she never would.

But part of her knew she already had.

Chapter Seven: The Matchbook

Callie didn't plan to stay after shift.

She hadn't brought extra snacks or a backup coffee. She didn't have clean scrubs for the next day or a reason to be lingering.

But her feet didn't take her to the exit.

They took her to the breakroom.

The last patient had been settled. Charting done. Her badge already tapped out. She could've gone home. Could've melted into the seat of her SUV and let the exhaustion claim her like always.

But she didn't.

Instead, she sat at the corner table in the flickering fluorescent haze and opened her notes app.

Blank screen.

Blank board.

Full heart.

She stared at the blinking cursor.

Not because she didn't know what to say.

Because once she said it, she couldn't unsay it.

The message came out faster than she expected. Her thumbs moved like they already knew.

> *The patient who died last week—her name was Dorothy Hennessy. She called me "sweetheart" and reminded me of my aunt. She coded alone because we were all in other rooms doing the impossible with not enough hands and not enough help. She wasn't the first. She won't be the last. But she was mine that day. And I can't pretend anymore.*

She paused.

Then added:

> *The next time someone asks why the nurses are so angry, feel free to hand them this.*

She saved it.

Then reopened it.

Then started something new.

It was small, at first. Just a list.

No names.

Just dates. Times. Bed numbers.

- **3/14** – 6 patients, no tech, missed pain med x3.

- **3/18** – IV infiltration not caught until rounds.

- **3/19** – Code Blue, cart uncharged. Dorothy.

She didn't know if it would become anything. But her body felt steadier writing it down. Like truth had mass, and she could carry it if she wrote it carefully enough.

At home, her youngest had fallen asleep with a toy truck tucked into the hood of his sweatshirt. Her oldest was curled up with his math book still open.

Callie kissed their foreheads and sat on the couch, phone glowing in the dark.

Her hand hovered over a group message. The one where the nurses shared memes and caffeine hacks and pictures of half-eaten donuts from the breakroom.

She started typing.

"What if we stopped waiting for change and started building it ourselves?"

She deleted it.

Typed again.

"Not a complaint. A record. Not gossip. A history. Not alone."

Still too much.

She backed out. Opened her notes again.

Scrolled to Dorothy's name.

Read it five times.

Then she created a new folder.

Title: The Matchbook

Inside, she dropped the log. The message. The pain.

She didn't post anything that night.

Didn't hit send.

But she started writing it all down.

And she saved it.

Because something was changing.

And she'd need the truth to light the way.

Chapter Eight: The First Flame

Callie didn't think anyone would scan it.

She printed the QR code in black and white, trimmed the edges, and taped it to the back of a clipboard no one ever used—the one buried behind the broken glucometer charger.

No logos. No names. Just a square of pixels and three words in plain font underneath:

Tell your story.

That's it.

No title. No campaign. No flashy pitch.

She didn't want to start a movement.

She just couldn't carry it all anymore.

She wanted to know she wasn't alone.

She'd created the form the night before, the house dark except for the screen glow and the rhythmic hum of the dryer in the hallway.

Question 1: What happened?
Question 2: When?
Question 3: What did you need that you didn't have?

Optional field: What would you say if no one could punish you for it?

At the top, she wrote:

> *This is anonymous. This is yours. No names. No rules. No apologies.*

She tested the form. Submitted a blank one to make sure it worked.

Then she stared at the screen for a long time.

Then she printed the code.

She left the first one in the staff bathroom, behind the extra gloves box. The second slid between two old charge forms on the med cart. The third—smallest, cleanest—was taped inside the breakroom cabinet where the forgotten Owalas and Stanleys lived, next to a faded sticky note that said *"Don't leave dirty dishes for the night shift, please."*

She didn't tell anyone.

She didn't need to.

The next day, after her shift, she checked the form.

12 responses.

One was blank.

Three were single sentences.

Eight were... heavy.

> *"My patient fell while I was in another room giving meds I wasn't trained for."*

> *"I have panic attacks before every shift. I keep a Zofran in my scrub pocket to dry-swallow before report."*

> *"I got written up for charting late. I was helping with a code across the hall. The manager never asked."*

She exhaled and closed the app.

The next morning, there were **34**.

By the end of the week: **over 100**.

Some were cold, clinical.

Others burned like open wounds.

Callie read every one.

She couldn't not.

At home, she sat at the kitchen table, the stories scrolling across her screen like confessionals. Her eyes were red. She hadn't blinked enough.

Her mom walked in holding a mug and paused.

Callie didn't look up.

"You okay?" her mom asked, though her voice was soft. Not pushing.

Callie didn't answer. She didn't need to.

Her mom set the mug down beside her—peppermint tea, no sugar—and slid into the chair across from her.

She didn't ask questions.

She just sat.

The screen kept glowing between them.

> *"They told me to smile more."*
> *"I watched a nurse cry alone in the med room. No one noticed."*
> *"I miss who I was before this job."*

That night, Callie sat alone in her room, the window cracked, cold air cutting through the silence.

She opened the form.

Scrolled to the bottom.

Clicked *Submit a Story*.

Her fingers hovered over the keyboard.

Then moved.

I used to love this work.
Now I leave every day wondering how many people I failed.
I tell my kids I'm tired because I didn't sleep.
I don't tell them I'm tired because I'm breaking.
We do not need pizza parties.
We need to be seen.
We need to be safe.
We need to be more than coverage.

She didn't sign it.

She didn't need to.

She hit send.

And for the first time, felt the heat in her chest burn steady.

Not panic.

Not despair.

Conviction.

She closed the laptop. Sat in the dark.

The air smelled like tea and the scent of her youngest's shampoo from his bedtime hug.

The flame didn't go out.

Chapter Nine: Smoke Signals

It started with a hallway comment.

"Did you read 137?" someone whispered near the med cart.

Callie kept her head down but clocked it.

"Had to be about this unit," another muttered.

By lunch, someone had printed a screenshot from the anonymous board and taped it behind the bathroom door.

> *"My hands shook so bad during med pass I dropped a vial. I told my preceptor I needed a second. She told me to 'push through.' I almost gave insulin to the wrong patient. No one ever reported it. I still see his face."*

The QR code had officially gone viral—at least inside these walls.

The stories were everywhere now. Whispered. Shared. Folded inside report sheets and scribbled on wiped whiteboards before huddle. Nurses were reading them between vitals, between meds, between moments of pretending everything was fine.

By the end of the week, the board had over 300 entries.

Not all long. Not all tragic.

But all true.

Monday morning, a new email hit inboxes.

> *To All Staff:*
>
> *It has come to our attention that an unauthorized, anonymous reporting platform has begun circulating digitally across clinical spaces. While we recognize the value of open dialogue, we must also prioritize professional standards and patient privacy.*
>
> *Please refrain from engaging with or promoting non-sanctioned communication channels.*

Callie read it three times.

It didn't say the stories were false.

It said they were *unauthorized*.

Jules found her at the nurse's station, sipping reheated coffee that tasted like stress and cardboard.

"You know you started this, right?"

Callie didn't look up. "What makes you think it was me?"

"Because it's good," Jules said. "And it's pissed off the exact right people."

Callie smiled behind the rim of her cup. "That's circumstantial."

In the breakroom, Tasha sat hunched over her phone, screen brightness dimmed.

"You think they can trace it?" she asked.

Callie shook her head. "It's anonymous. I didn't—whoever started it—didn't use names."

Tasha gave her a look that said she already knew. Then whispered, "Be careful, okay?"

Lucy, the CNA, found her outside Room 306 later that day. She didn't say much. Just handed her a folded slip of paper.

Callie opened it later.

Some of us thought we were the only ones.
Thank you for making it less lonely.

At the end of the shift, Dana, the charge nurse, cornered Callie by the clean supply closet.

"We got flagged for a rounding log again," Dana said, voice clipped. "Leadership's poking around."

Callie nodded slowly. "Let me guess. They care more about that than the fact we've been short four nights in a row."

Dana didn't confirm. But her eyes did.

Then she added, quietly, "You didn't hear it from me, but… the stories? Some of us are reading them in admin meetings."

Callie blinked.

"You'd be surprised who's listening," Dana said.

Then she walked away.

She almost made it out of the building before her name came over the intercom.

"Callie Harper, please report to Clinical Administration."

Her stomach dropped.

The office was sterile. Fake plants. Abstract prints. Carpet that muffled everything like secrets.

The woman waiting for her was from HR. Maybe Risk. It didn't matter.

She offered tea Callie didn't want and a seat Callie didn't need.

"We just wanted to check in," she said with a practiced smile. "There's been a lot of… chatter. We understand tensions are high."

Callie said nothing.

The woman leaned forward.

> "Sometimes speaking out has unintended consequences. We just want to make sure everyone remembers the importance of professionalism."

Callie raised an eyebrow. "Is that a threat?"

"Of course not," the woman said quickly. "We're simply asking for cooperation."

Callie stood.

"Then I'll keep cooperating. Like I always have. Like every nurse here does—until it kills them."

She walked out.

Didn't slam the door.

Didn't need to.

Back in the breakroom, someone had taped up a new message beside the microwave.

Sharpie on printer paper. All caps.

> *THEY CAN THROW WATER ON A FIRE.*

> *STILL, EMBERS BURN*

Callie stood there, still in her scrubs, sweat-dried and aching.

She didn't add anything.

Didn't need to.

She just smiled.

—————————-

Anonymous Submission

Posted anonymously. Timestamped 2:14 a.m.

I was four weeks off orientation.

Med-Surg. Night shift.

My patient was circling the drain—BP unreadable, O2 in the 70s, GCS tanking fast.

I hit the rapid response button.

Nothing.

Charge was in a staffing meeting.

RT was stuck on another floor.

The resident was asleep and couldn't be paged "unless vitals were critical."

They were.

But no one came.

I started compressions. Alone.

Did my best until help finally showed—eleven minutes later.

We got him back.

He never woke up.

I still see his face.

Still hear the silence when I called for help.

They said I "managed the situation well."

But that's not what I did.

Chapter Ten: Backdraft

The QR board had become a monster.

Not a loud one—but a steady, breathing thing. It lived under the surface of everything now.

Over 600 entries.

Some just a sentence.
Some pages long.
Some written like rage in a bottle.
Others like eulogies.

Every floor whispered about it. Every nurse read it— even if they swore they didn't. Callie had watched a charge nurse pull it up between call lights. Watched a night tech screenshot one and send it to herself like a confession she couldn't make out loud.

And admin?

Admin had gone quiet.

Which meant they were planning something.

She got the message after shift, scribbled on the corner of a transport form and folded into the bottom of her bag.

Garage. 9 p.m. Bring no expectations.

No name. Just a time and a location—Melissa's garage, if Callie had to guess. No one called it that out loud. But Melissa had the kind of driveway that wrapped like a hug and the kind of heart that didn't flinch when things got messy.

When Callie pulled up, the garage door was already halfway open.

Inside were folding chairs, a cooler with dollar-store sparkling water, and a whiteboard leaning against a rake.

Melissa stood off to the side, hoodie over her scrubs, arms crossed in that way she did when she was holding both grace and fury in the same breath.

She smiled when she saw Callie. "Didn't know if you'd come."

Callie shrugged. "Didn't know if I'd want to talk."

"That's okay," Melissa said. "Listening counts."

There were five of them at first.

Melissa. Jules. Callie. A quiet telemetry nurse whose name Callie didn't catch. And Kayla.

Kayla looked exactly how Callie remembered her—hair pulled back tight, nails immaculate, badge clipped straight. Still sharp. Still fast. The kind of nurse who knew who to cc on emails and which committee seats led to the best day shifts.

But something had shifted. A crack in the performance. Her voice didn't carry the same shine when she spoke.

"They're saying the forum is a violation," Kayla said, voice low. "That it's dangerous. That it's... inciting distrust."

Jules snorted. "Distrust was already there. The forum just turned the lights on."

Kayla didn't argue.

She just looked tired.

Callie watched her. Watched the wheels turning. The conflict. The need to believe in the ladder she'd been climbing—and the ache of realizing the rungs might be broken.

They talked around the issue for a while.

Ratios. Policies. The silent retaliation happening in the form of floating assignments and schedule reshuffles.

Then Melissa stepped forward, pulled a folder from her bag, and dropped it on the table.

"Stories," she said. "Hard copies. Ones they'll delete if we let them live only online."

Callie flipped through one.

It wasn't hers.

But it could've been.

"What's the plan?" someone asked.

Everyone looked at Callie.

She blinked. "What? Why are you all looking at me?"

Jules grinned. "Because you're the one who lit the damn match. We're just following the smoke."

Callie leaned back in her chair, arms crossed, mouth pressed into a line.

"I didn't want this," she said.

Melissa nodded. "Doesn't mean you're not the one for it."

Kayla looked at her then. Really looked.

"You're not the loudest," she said. "But you're the one we listen to."

It wasn't praise. It was permission.

And it landed heavy.

They stayed until almost midnight.

The conversation shifted from stories to structure.

What came next.
 Who would write the letter.
 Whether they'd sign names.
 Whether they'd risk anything at all.

And Callie?

She didn't make promises.

But she didn't leave early either.

When she got home, the house was dark. Her mom had left the porch light on. Her oldest's math book still sat open on the table.

Callie stood at the sink, staring out the kitchen window into the quiet.

She could still smell hospital soap on her hands.

Still hear Jules laughing softly in that garage. Melissa saying "we'll protect each other." Kayla whispering, "I don't know if I'm brave enough."

Callie didn't know if she was either.

But she *was* tired enough. Angry enough. *Done* enough.

She grabbed her laptop.

Opened a blank doc.

Typed:

> *We are not just coverage.*
> *We are not just labor.*
> *We are not shadows, or silence, or staff-to-be-flexed.*
> *We are the system's spine.*
> *And it has forgotten who holds it up.*

She stared at it.

Then saved the file:

Backdraft Manifesto - Draft 1

Chapter Eleven: The Line in the Floor

The shift started with a new poster taped to the breakroom door.

> *TOWN HALL: Building Trust Through Communication*
> *Mandatory Attendance – All Clinical Staff*
> *Friday. 3 p.m. Conference Room A.*

Below it, someone had written in Sharpie:

> **Translation: Sit down, shut up, and smile.**

By noon, the comment was gone. But everyone had seen it.

They made their move the day before the meeting.

The email hit the staff inboxes like a stun grenade:

> *As part of our commitment to a safe and professional environment, we have placed a staff member on administrative leave pending review of conduct related to unauthorized disclosures and the spread of misinformation.*

No name.

But by the time Callie hit her lunch break, the whispers had a face.

Kayla.

Callie found her in the stairwell. Third floor. Near the vending machine that never worked.

Kayla didn't cry. She just sat on the concrete steps, holding her ID badge like it might unlock some other version of the day.

"They said I was sowing distrust," she said, voice flat. "That I'd been seen associating with the wrong people too many times. That I made leadership look negligent."

Callie sat beside her.

"I didn't even post anything," Kayla whispered. "I just... read."

"Doesn't matter," Callie said quietly. "They're trying to scare the rest of us."

Kayla laughed—sharp, bitter. "Then it's working."

That night, the garage meeting doubled in size.

Tasha came, silent but present. A new grad from Telemetry. A float nurse who hadn't spoken until she blurted, "I can't sleep the night before my shift anymore."

Melissa brought laminated cards—QR codes linking to safe copies of the board, saved externally.

Jules brought her speaker and a playlist titled *"Revolution Vibes: Sad but Also Ready to Burn It Down."*

Callie didn't speak until the end.

Everyone was spinning about the town hall. About Kayla.

They were afraid.

And she was too.

But she also knew what it felt like to stay quiet—and she was done with that.

She stood.

Not tall. Not loud.

But solid.

"If they want to draw a line," she said, "then we decide if we step over it together—or one by one."

No one clapped.

But no one moved either.

And in the quiet that followed, something held.

The next day, Conference Room A was packed.

Every chair was filled. Staff lined up along the back wall. Scrub colors like protest flags.

Admin stood at the front in suits.

The EHR screen behind them said *"Trust & Transparency"* in pale blue font.

The Chief Nursing Officer opened with a smile that didn't meet her eyes.

"We know there have been concerns."

Someone coughed.

"We want to reestablish open communication."

Callie watched the room. Saw Tasha gripping her pen like it was armor. Melissa with arms folded, eyes flinty. Jules... smiling too much. Dangerous.

Then the CNO said:

"Let's hear from the floor. Who wants to speak?"

No one moved.

Then a chair scraped the tile.

Callie stood.

She didn't raise her voice.

Didn't point fingers.

Didn't name Kayla.

She just said:

> "We don't need another poster. We need a reason to believe the next Dorothy won't die the same way."

The room went still.

The admin team didn't respond right away.

Then someone cleared their throat.

"Well," said a man in a grey suit, "that's certainly a powerful anecdote."

Callie blinked.

Jules muttered, "Wrong answer."

Melissa leaned forward in her chair.

And just like that, the line was visible.

Drawn sharp across the room.

After the meeting, Callie didn't feel brave.

She felt... exposed.

But when she got back to the unit, someone had written on the whiteboard outside the breakroom:

One voice broke the silence today.

Below it, someone else had added:

Let's not make her stand there alone.

Chapter Twelve: Pressure Points

The next shift felt like a warning shot.

The whiteboards had been wiped clean before anyone clocked in. The bulletin board outside the breakroom now displayed a freshly laminated copy of the hospital's **"Code of Conduct."**

Someone had replaced the microwave sticky note with a typed message:

> *"All employees are reminded to maintain a professional attitude when engaging in internal and external communications. Including social media."*

Nobody said QR code.

But everyone heard it.

Jules caught Callie at the med fridge.

"You good?"

Callie shrugged. "Define good."

Jules opened her coffee thermos and dumped in a sugar packet like she was fueling for war. "You stood up in a room full of suits and said Dorothy's name out loud.

You shook something loose. Just making sure it didn't shake you, too."

Callie leaned on the counter. "I didn't mean to speak."

"Yeah, but you did," Jules said. "And it hit. You're louder than you think, Callie."

They passed each other all shift, tossing meds and sarcasm back and forth like old times. But underneath it, Callie felt the pull.

Jules wasn't just watching her.

She was *tracking* her.

The way a mentor watches their pupil not because they doubt—but because they *know what's coming next* and want them to survive it.

Kayla showed up on the unit two hours into shift.

Not in scrubs. In black slacks and a tight, blank expression.

She walked like her badge still had weight, but her hands stayed in her pockets.

Callie found her standing outside Room 308, looking at the board, but not really reading it.

"They let you back?" Callie asked.

Kayla shook her head. "Clearance meeting. Observational review. Whatever the hell that means."

A pause.

"I'm not sure I can stay," Kayla added. "Not because I don't care. But because I care too much. And this place eats that for breakfast."

Callie nodded. "You don't have to choose today."

Kayla's laugh was small, sad. "I do, actually. I've been climbing a ladder I think might be duct-taped to the ceiling."

And then came Rhonda.

Badge clipped sideways. Purple scrubs with cartoon owls. Hair in a bun that had *definitely* lost the war hours ago.

She blew into the breakroom like she owned it.

"I swear to God," she announced, "if one more person tells me to smile, I'm gonna tattoo patient satisfaction scores on my ass and moon for the next Joint Commission audit."

Callie choked on her coffee.

Jules raised her cup. "Welcome back, Rhonda."

"Was I gone?"

"You've been too quiet lately."

Rhonda dropped into a chair. "That's because I've been waiting for someone to actually burn this place down. But now that the fires have started? Consider me unsupervised and deeply motivated."

They laughed.

The real kind. The kind that shakes out of your chest like a cough you didn't know you needed.

Rhonda pointed her coffee stirrer at Callie. "You're the match, huh?"

Callie blinked. "Excuse me?"

"You lit the board. You poked the bear. You said Dorothy's name in front of God and middle management."

"I didn't mean—"

"Stop. Own it. You didn't mean to start something, but you *did*. And now that you've broken the silence, the rest of us are gonna follow it right to the edge."

Callie leaned back.

It wasn't praise.

It was permission.

That evening, another post appeared on the anonymous board:

> *"They threatened to trace us. But they can't unhear us."*

Callie didn't write it.

But she felt it, like it was branded to her ribs.

Later, in the parking garage, she ran into Melissa.

They stood between their cars, doors open, air heavy.

"You okay?" Melissa asked.

"No," Callie said. "But I'm not alone."

Melissa smiled. "Exactly."

As they were about to part, Melissa hesitated.

"By the way… next week? We're not just meeting in the garage."

Callie raised an eyebrow.

"We're taking it off the floor," Melissa said. "Someone's offered us space. A place to speak with no badges. No scrub colors. No policy binders."

"What's it for?"

Melissa looked her dead in the eye.

> "It's time we stopped collecting stories and started deciding what to *do* with them."

Callie didn't answer right away.

But she knew one thing:

The pressure had stopped pushing her down.

Now it was pressing her forward.

Chapter 12.5 – The Listening Door

Callie was ten the first time she realized her mom lied after work.

Not big lies.

Not fairy tales.

Just enough smoothing around the edges to make dinner happen without scaring anyone.

But Callie had heard the door slam when her mom got home.

Had watched the way her hands shook, pouring iced tea.

Had seen the dried bloodstain on the left sleeve of her scrubs—wiped but not gone.

She started listening at the door after that.

Not on purpose.

It just… happened.

She'd sit in the hallway at night, knees pulled to her chest, ear near the cracked bedroom door while her mom vented to no one.

> "She was twenty. And alone.
> The doc didn't even look at her before calling it."
> "I told them she was crashing. They didn't believe me until the monitor flatlined."
> "I'm so tired of being right after i

Callie didn't understand everything she heard.

But she understood enough.

There was a world inside that hospital.

One where adults didn't always win.

Where people bled out not because of bad luck, but because no one listened fast enough.

One night, her mom muttered something she'd never forget.

> "Some things you carry in silence.
> Because saying them out loud means admitting no one came to help."

Callie didn't sleep much that night.

And by morning?

She'd already decided two things:

1. She was going to be a nurse.

2. She was going to talk louder than the silence ever could.

Chapter Thirteen: The Echo Room

Melissa's garage was never meant to hold a revolution.

It had started with five people, a cooler of sparkling water, and a whiteboard propped against a rake. But now? The stories had grown legs. And the crowd had doubled. Then tripled.

So when an old nurse—retired, sharp as ever—offered up the basement of her church, no questions asked, they said yes.

No one called it a movement.

Not out loud.

But Callie could feel it in her bones the second she walked into that dim, echoey space with folding chairs and mismatched thermoses.

They were here for something more than venting.

They were here to decide what came next.

Callie slipped into the room wearing jeans, a hoodie, and the kind of exhaustion that no sleep could fix.

The lights were soft. The chairs were full. And the walls buzzed—not from machines, but from voices.

She spotted Melissa first, handing out paper copies of a story archive.

Jules leaned against a post near the back, arms crossed, smirking like she was already five steps ahead of the plan.

Tasha waved her over. She looked less nervous here. Like she could breathe.

And then—Rhonda, in her full uncensored glory, waving a finger in someone's face.

"I'm just saying," she barked, "if they're gonna hand out pizza during Nurse Appreciation Week, the least they can do is not poison us with crust that tastes like sadness and chart audits."

Callie raised an eyebrow. "Is that today's agenda? Revenge on the pizza cartel?"

Rhonda grinned. "You bring the revolution. I'll bring the snacks."

The chairs were arranged in a loose circle. Not quite therapy. Not quite strategy. Just... real.

A nurse Callie didn't know stood and cleared her throat.

"We've all read the stories. We've lived them. But we can't keep hiding behind anonymity if we want change."

The room held its breath.

Then someone else added, "We don't all have to go public. But someone has to. Someone they'll listen to."

And every head—slowly, almost guiltily—turned to Callie.

She blinked. "Don't all volunteer me at once."

Jules chuckled. "You already did, babe. You just didn't know it."

Callie stood, eventually. Not because she wanted to. Because she knew she had to.

She didn't raise her voice.

She didn't rehearse.

She just told the truth.

"I didn't mean to start anything," she said. "I was just tired of bleeding quietly. Tired of losing patients and coworkers and pieces of myself while being told to smile and update the whiteboard."

A few nods. One muttered "hell yes."

"I'm not brave," she added. "I'm pissed off. There's a difference."

Someone clapped.

Callie held up a hand. "Don't clap. I'm still on the fence about puking."

Laughter.

She let it land.

"But since we're all here," she continued, "let's stop waiting for someone else to fix it. Let's decide what *we* want. What we demand. And how loud we're willing to get."

After, she found Kayla sitting alone in the back corner.

Not in scrubs. In leggings and a plain sweatshirt. Her hair down. No armor.

"You came," Callie said.

Kayla nodded. "I'm not sure what I'm doing here."

Callie sat beside her. "Half of us aren't. We just knew we couldn't not show up."

Kayla looked down. "They offered me a meeting with HR. Said if I apologized for 'disruption,' they'd let me keep my status."

"And?"

"I didn't answer."

Callie grinned, just a little. "That's a shame. Would've loved to see you turn that meeting into a TED Talk on institutional gaslighting."

Kayla smirked. "Don't tempt me."

Later, as the meeting broke into groups, Jules sidled up to Callie.

"You're doing it."

Callie raised an eyebrow. "Doing what?"

"Becoming the problem they didn't plan for."

Callie sipped from a half-warm coffee and glanced around the room.

Fifty nurses. Four CNAs. Two respiratory techs. One retired director of nursing taking notes in a spiral-bound notebook labeled *'In Case We Torch It All.'*

"I don't want to lead," she said.

Jules bumped her shoulder. "You don't have to want it. You just have to not run."

Callie let out a long breath.

"I've spent years swallowing fire," she said.

"Yeah?" Jules replied. "Maybe it's time you started breathing it out."

As they packed up for the night, someone taped a new sheet to the wall near the light switch.

> *We are not anonymous anymore.*
> *We are accountable.*
> *And we are here.*

Callie stared at it as the room emptied.

She didn't add anything.

But she didn't look away.

Chapter Fourteen: The First Name

The manifesto was printed on plain paper.

No header. No logo. Just a stack of stapled pages shoved inside an old manila folder like it might catch fire if anyone looked too long.

Callie stared at the title.

WE ARE THE SYSTEM'S SPINE.

Underneath, the first line:

> *This is not a threat. It's a pulse check.*

The room was quiet, but not still. The kind of quiet that vibrated with suppressed panic and coffee-fueled resolve.

They were back in the echo room—twice as many chairs this time, and none of them empty.

Someone passed out pens.

Callie held hers like a weapon.

Melissa read the document aloud. Not performative. Not passionate. Just steady, like a heartbeat.

It covered everything:

- Unsafe ratios.

- Retaliation disguised as reassignment.

- The deaths they weren't allowed to grieve.

- The policies signed by people who hadn't touched a patient since Y2K.

And then it asked for what they deserved:

- A seat at the table.

- A voice in staffing.

- Real trauma support.

- A public acknowledgement of what had been lost.

At the bottom of the last page, a single line waited.

Name (optional):

The room held its breath.

Someone coughed. A folding chair creaked. Somewhere in the back, Rhonda muttered, "Optional my ass."

Callie didn't move.

Her hands stayed in her lap, pen frozen.

She could feel eyes shifting toward her—some subtle, some not.

Jules, sitting across the circle, gave her a look like *you don't have to—but if you do, we'll follow.*

Callie didn't want to.

She wanted to go back to being a ghost in the breakroom, sipping cold coffee and rolling her eyes at policy emails.

But then she thought about Dorothy.
 About the crash cart that didn't charge.
 About Kayla, folded in on herself in that stairwell.
 About the CNA who handed her a thank-you note with trembling fingers and said, "For seeing me."

She stood.

No big speech. No power pose.

Just her, a folding chair, and a pen.

She walked to the table, scrawled her name on the bottom of the document, and said—loud enough for the back row to hear:

"I'm not doing this because I'm fearless. I'm doing it because I'm *fucking* tired."

Then she walked back to her seat.

And the room exhaled.

Melissa signed next. Jules followed. Tasha, lips trembling but eyes steel, added hers like a whisper.

Rhonda paused at the paper, popped her gum, and muttered, "Well, they already hate me. Might as well make it official."

Afterward, the manifesto was tucked into a plastic binder and slid into Melissa's bag.

They didn't say what came next.

They didn't have to.

They'd crossed the line.

No take-backs.

Callie left late, last out the door.

As she stepped into the night air, someone called after her.

"Hey."

She turned. It was Kayla, holding her own copy of the manifesto in one hand.

"I haven't signed yet," she said.

"You don't have to."

Kayla looked down. "Yeah. But I think I need to."

A pause.

Then Kayla added, "You scared?"

Callie's smile was tired. Wry. Wounded.

"Terrified."

Kayla nodded. "Good. Means you're not numb."

That night, back at home, Callie sat on the floor of her bedroom with her laptop glowing in her lap.

She opened the anonymous board.

Scrolled past dozens of new entries.

At the top was one pinned message, recently posted:

Callie Harper signed first.

Her chest went cold.

She didn't post it. She hadn't told anyone.

But someone had.

And now it was out there.

She stared at the screen.

No turning back.

No silence to hide in.

Just her name.

At the top of the list.

And a match in her hand.

———-

Internal Memo – REDACTED

Leaked to Anonymous board.

Origin: Risk Management Division.

Subject:

Re: Language Protocol – Adverse Events Reporting

Team,

As a reminder:

- All adverse events must be reviewed by administrative liaison prior to Risk submission.

- The word "harm" is not to be used in preliminary drafts.

- Use language such as "unanticipated outcome" or "post-procedural shift in baseline."

- Do not reference staffing levels in event documentation.

- If the event involves a patient's death, notify Legal immediately before notifying the family.

Do not speculate. Do not editorialize. Do not escalate.

Thank you for your discretion.

"This is not documentation. It's self-preservation."

— handwritten in the margin, unknown author

Chapter Fifteen: The Reckoning Memo

"Off the record… do you believe it can actually change?"

Raine Ellis didn't do fluff.

No sponsored content. No clickbait. No "10 Things Nurses Love About New Scrubs" garbage.

She wrote what bled. What got buried. What made PR teams sweat through their button-downs.

She'd covered rural maternal care collapses, inner-city ER shutdowns, and one particularly nasty exposé on a for-profit hospice network that had filed two lawsuits and a restraining order against her. She framed the restraining order.

But this?

This had a different smell.

Not a scandal. *Movement.*

The QR board had caught her attention three weeks ago.

An anonymous nurse had DM'd her a link with no context. Just:

"You want the truth? Try listening here."

At first, Raine thought it was a prank.

But then she started reading.

Dozens of entries. Hundreds. No hashtags. No branding. Just story after story—raw, cracked, real.

By the time she hit entry #412—*"I keep a Zofran in my pocket just so I don't puke before shift"*—she knew it wasn't isolated.

It was *boiling*.

She was still scanning new submissions when her burner line buzzed.

Only a handful of people had this number.

The message read:

> *Check your email. Callie Harper. Manifesto attached. She didn't write it alone. But her name's the first.*
> *The next Echo Room is tonight. You didn't hear it from me.*
> —M.

Raine didn't have to ask who M was.

She'd been feeding her whispers for months.

A per diem nurse. Smart. Strategic. Untouchable because she was everywhere—and technically nowhere.

Raine opened the PDF.

The manifesto read like a battle hymn:

> *We are not coverage.*
> *We are not liability shields.*
> *We are the spine of this system, and we*
> *will no longer bear its weight alone.*

At the bottom: Callie Harper.

And three more names. All verified. All still working.

It wasn't just a complaint.

It was *organized defiance.*

And if what M said was true, they were about to meet. In person. In a basement. Tonight.

The building was low brick, plain, and church-owned. The kind of place where NA meetings happened and folding chairs outnumbered prayers.

Raine slipped in quietly, dressed down in jeans and a black zip-up. She didn't bring a recorder. Just a worn leather notebook and a mechanical pencil.

Inside, the air buzzed like static.

Forty people. No scrubs. But Callie's face was unmistakable—pulled back hair, navy hoodie, hands wrapped around a coffee she clearly wasn't drinking.

She wasn't loud. But when she spoke, the room *moved*.

Raine watched. Listened. Took notes in shorthand.

Someone stood near the front, holding the latest hospital-wide memo like it was radioactive.

> *We discourage anonymous platforms that may misrepresent the experiences of our dedicated clinical staff…*

It was the corporate version of, *"Shut up or else."*

But no one was shutting up.

Rhonda—Raine didn't know her name yet, but she'd remember her—stood up and said, "They want professionalism? Let's mail them a bedpan with a copy of the billable hours we waste cleaning up their negligence."

Laughter. Applause. A crackle of courage.

After the meeting, Raine waited outside the building, leaning against the brick with her hands in her jacket pockets.

She didn't approach Callie.

Callie approached her.

"You a reporter?"

Raine smiled. "Guess I'm not as subtle as I thought."

Callie didn't smile back. Just studied her for a long second.

"You here to make us look stupid?"

"No," Raine said. "I'm here to tell the truth. Your kind of truth. The dangerous kind."

A pause. A shift.

Callie crossed her arms.

"Off the record," Raine added, "do you believe it can actually change?"

Callie exhaled, slow and tight.

"I don't know," she said. "But I know silence won't save us."

Raine nodded. "Then let's start there."

Chapter 15.5 – Not Your Story

The Interview

Raine hit record.

Not in a dramatic way. No click. No warning.

Just a quiet shift in the room that Callie felt before she heard it.

They were in the garage.

Concrete and chill.

The kind of space where revolution wasn't symbolic—it was survival.

Raine sat across from her, laptop open, posture neutral.

Too neutral.

The kind that says I'm listening, but also framing this already.

"You've become a symbol," Raine said.
"Even if you didn't ask to be."

Callie didn't blink.

"Symbols don't get CPS at their door."

Raine exhaled. Not annoyed—just calibrated.

"That's exactly why people need to hear it."
"Then write the truth. Not a headline."
"I'm not twisting anything."

Callie leaned forward.

"You're writing a story. That means you're
choosing a hero. A villain. A climax.
But this isn't a movie, Raine. This is Tuesday."

Silence stretched.

Not heavy.

Sharp.

Raine looked away for the first time. Then back.

"You think I don't get that?"

Callie said nothing.

Raine closed the laptop. Slowly.

"My sister's a nurse. Burned out. On Lexapro and caffeine and one shift away from not coming home.

I'm not here to sell your story, Callie.

I'm here because maybe if I help the world see you, she'll believe someone might see her."

Callie's breath caught.

Not from anger.

From something deeper.

Something recognition-shaped.

She looked down. Then back up.

"Then stop writing about me.
Write about what they built that made me necessary."

Raine nodded.

Pressed record again.

But this time?

She didn't say a word.

Chapter Sixteen: The Bridge Burned Both Ways

The email subject line read: **"Leadership Opportunity – Internal Liaison Pilot Program."**

Kayla stared at it so long she forgot to blink.

> *We believe your professionalism, reliability, and familiarity with staff concerns make you an ideal candidate for this vital bridge-building role…*

There it was.

The ladder.

Still standing.

Still shiny.

Still climbing directly over a pile of broken bodies.

She didn't answer. Not yet.

But she didn't delete it either.

And that was the problem.

Across the building, Callie sat outside the stairwell exit, sipping bad coffee and watching her breath curl into the cold.

The Echo Room meetings had gone from underground to standing-room-only.

The QR board had gone from secret to unstoppable.

And Raine Ellis had gone from a quiet maybe to a definite *problem*—at least from the hospital's perspective.

Not that Callie had said much to her since that first post-meeting conversation.

But she could feel the pressure building behind the scenes.

Like the next move was coming. And it was going to hit hard.

The memo dropped Thursday morning.

Not just an internal communication—this one made the press.

A polished, lawyered-up press release from the hospital:

> *"We do not support or condone the unauthorized sharing of internal*

*experiences without context or verification.
We remain committed to safety, growth, and
professionalism. Any employee who
participates in media engagement without
formal clearance may face administrative
review."*

Translation: *We're watching you. And we're ready to
swing.*

Callie read it in the breakroom.

Jules walked in and read it over her shoulder.

"That sounds like a threat dressed up in HR drag."

Callie snorted. "It's giving 'bully in a blazer.'"

Jules leaned on the counter. "You heard about Kayla?"

Callie froze. "No. What?"

"They offered her the liaison role."

Of course they did.

Of course they would toss her a bone just big enough to
buy her silence.

Callie found Kayla later that day in the stairwell between floors—same place they'd collided weeks before when Dorothy died.

Kayla looked like hell. Wrinkled blazer. Hair pinned too tight. Badge hanging crooked.

"You going to take it?" Callie asked, straight out.

Kayla didn't pretend not to know what she meant.

She hesitated.

"They say I can help. That I can be a voice for both sides."

Callie raised an eyebrow. "Yeah? And which side do you whisper for when they gag the other one?"

Silence.

Then softer:

"They'll listen to me," Kayla said, like she was trying to convince herself. "Maybe I can keep you from getting fired."

Callie laughed. Once. Bitter.

"Sweetheart, I already lit the match. The only thing left to decide is who's standing beside me when the smoke clears."

She turned to leave.

Kayla didn't follow.

That night, in the Echo Room, the tension was different.

Not fear.

Not fury.

Something colder.

Resolved.

Jules had spread copies of the press release on the table.

Melissa was circling phrases with a red pen like a prosecutor.

Tasha stood near the corner, typing into her phone with a set jaw.

Even Rhonda was quiet—which was how Callie knew it was real.

Then Raine walked in.

She didn't say anything at first.

Just dropped a folder on the table.

Inside: a draft.

"Dying on the Clock: Inside the Collapse of the American Nurse."

Callie flipped through it. Her name wasn't on the byline.

But her fingerprints were all over the fire.

Raine looked at her and said, "You have final review, before it goes live."

Callie stared at the folder.

Then nodded.

The next morning, Kayla's name appeared in the hospital-wide newsletter.

Clinical Staff Liaison – Pilot Program Announced.

Callie didn't say anything.

She didn't have to.

The bridge had burned.

And the smoke was finally reaching the top floor.

Chapter Seventeen: Smoke in the Lungs

The article went live at 8:42 a.m.

By 9:03, the QR code was trending.

By noon, hospital leadership had called an emergency meeting.

And by 4:00 p.m., Callie's name had been mentioned in three national nursing groups, one Reddit thread titled *"Holy Hell, This Nurse Said What We're All Thinking"*, and an email from legal marked **Confidential.**

She hadn't even had lunch.

Raine hadn't warned her before publishing.

But she didn't need to.

Callie had read the draft.

She'd said yes.

Even when her hands shook.

Even when Jules had whispered, *"Once it's out, you can't take it back."*

Callie had looked her in the eye and replied, "Good."

The headline hit like a punch:

Dying on the Clock: One Nurse's Unfiltered Truth About a Healthcare System in Collapse
By Raine Ellis

It wasn't just a piece.

It was an indictment.

QR codes embedded in the article led directly to the anonymous board. By lunchtime, they were screen-shotted, printed, slapped onto breakroom fridges and bathroom stalls across state lines.

Some were scrawled on sticky notes.

Others turned into sharp, clean fliers with bold text:

SCAN. READ. BELIEVE US.

The stories flooded in faster than the system could hide them.

And this time, there were names.

Not just nurses.

Patients. Families. Techs. Therapists. Interns.

Callie sat in her car outside the hospital, phone buzzing non-stop.

Texts. Emails. Two voicemails from blocked numbers.

One was her old preceptor from her very first med-surg job.

> "Is this really you? Jesus, Harper. I'm proud of you. And scared for you."

The second was shorter.

> "They're going to come for you now. Be ready."

Inside, the mood had changed.

Not loud.

Not even angry.

Watchful.

Admin walked through the halls with clipboards again.

Managers huddled behind closed doors.

But nurses?

They were *talking*.

Openly.

In corners. At desks. Mid-shift.

Even Rhonda kept her voice down—but her words still cut like scalpels.

> "They've been bleeding us dry for years.
> Now we're hemorrhaging the truth and they
> can't find the clamp."

In the breakroom, someone had printed out the article's first paragraph and taped it to the wall.

Underneath, someone else had added in red marker:

> ***"We told you. You didn't listen. So now
> we're speaking louder."***

Callie didn't know who wrote it.

But she felt it in her lungs.

Thick. Heavy. Real.

Like smoke you couldn't cough out.

She found Kayla near the stairwell again.

This time, she didn't wait.

"They're spinning it," Callie said flatly. "Calling it exaggerated. Accusing Raine of bias."

Kayla looked exhausted. But not defensive.

"They asked me to give a quote," she said.

Callie raised an eyebrow. "Let me guess. Something professional. Polished. Empty."

"I didn't say yes."

Callie waited.

Kayla didn't look away.

"I didn't say no, either," she added.

Callie nodded slowly.

"Then make a choice, Kayla. But make it fast. The fire's already here."

That night, back in the Echo Room, the energy was nuclear.

Everyone had seen the article.

Most had shared it.

A few had family members text them crying. Others had old coworkers reach out with apologies and solidarity.

Tasha stood near the projector, reading new submissions.

Jules had a legal pad with three columns: protect, escalate, document.

Melissa sat in the corner, silent, jaw tight. Watching everyone.

And Callie?

She walked to the center.

Cleared her throat.

And said the only thing left:

> "We started this as a whisper.
> Now it's a reckoning.
> So let's stop surviving it—and start steering it."

The room didn't clap.

They *stood*.

Archived Headline – *Not for Distribution*

NURSE TERMINATED AFTER REPORTING UNSAFE STAFFING – CASE SETTLED, GAG ORDER ISSUED

Byline: Investigative Desk | March 12

Redacted Media Network

A former ICU nurse employed by [Hospital System Name Redacted] was terminated days after submitting a formal report citing repeated unsafe staffing ratios, patient delays in care, and a pattern of managerial retaliation.

Legal proceedings were initiated, then sealed.

The nurse, represented by [Redacted], accepted a confidential settlement and is no longer practicing bedside care.

Neither the hospital nor the nurse are permitted to speak further under the terms of the resolution.

A public statement issued by the facility reads:

"We value all staff concerns and take safety seriously."

No comment was given on whether corrective actions were taken.

"I didn't sign the gag order because I wanted to. I signed it because I needed to eat."
— Anonymous message received via Anonymous board

Chapter Eighteen: The Exit Interview

They didn't fire her.

They reassigned her.

Which, in nurse speak, meant: *"We can't prove anything yet, but we want you gone."*

Her name wasn't on the press release.

But every nurse on the floor knew what it meant when Leah from nights was suddenly "transitioning to a non-patient-facing administrative capacity effective immediately."

She hadn't even posted a story.

All she'd done was *like* the article on her personal Facebook.

Twice.

Callie found out in the med room, via whisper.

Jules confirmed it fifteen minutes later with a single text:

JULES: *They're testing us. If we stay quiet while they make her the example, they'll come for the rest of us next.*

CALLIE: *So we get louder?*

JULES: *We get smarter.*

Raine texted next.

RAINE: *Are you okay with the follow-up focusing on retaliation? I've already got three off-the-record confirmations from other nurses.*

CALLIE: *Make it hit. No names from the board unless they gave them. They're not collateral.*

RAINE: *You're protecting people who wouldn't blink before throwing you under a bus.*

CALLIE: *That's the difference between me and the system.*

The next Echo Room meeting started differently.

Melissa didn't open with a recap.

She just stood and said, "We lost Leah."

Rhonda muttered, "They didn't fire her. They ghosted her with paperwork."

Callie nodded. "She's gone. Let's not pretend otherwise."

Kayla was there too.

Quiet. Present. Still trying to bridge something that had already burned.

Callie caught her eye.

Kayla looked away.

Someone had printed out a new QR story and pinned it to the corkboard near the coffee pot.

> *"They tell us to use the chain of command. But when the chain is rusted through, it only breaks us faster."*

It had no name.

But everyone in the room knew it came from one of their own.

Later that night, Callie sat at the kitchen table, a pile of worksheets beside her and the hum of the fridge as her only soundtrack.

Her oldest son looked up from his homework and asked, "Did you make that story thing online?"

Callie blinked. "What do you mean?"

"Someone at school said their mom scanned a code and read about a nurse who said no one listens until someone dies."

Callie closed her laptop.

Carefully.

Quietly.

"Sometimes people say hard things because no one else will," she said.

He didn't push. Just nodded.

But he was watching her now—different.

Like he knew his mom was someone the world was starting to notice.

The next day, Callie was pulled into a meeting.

Not Risk.

Not HR.

Just "a conversation" with a leadership rep whose name she didn't know and whose tie looked like it had been ironed into submission.

He didn't threaten her.

Didn't raise his voice.

But his smile was the kind that came with handcuffs made of policy.

> "We just want to understand where all this unrest is coming from."

Callie smiled back.

"Then maybe try listening when people speak."

When she walked out, Jules was waiting by the elevator.

"Well?" she asked.

Callie smirked. "They want me to believe they're building bridges."

"And?"

"I told them I already burned mine."

Chapter 18.5 – The Door She Didn't Open

Kayla stood outside the Quality Office holding a manila folder like it was a live wire.

Inside:

- Two falsified vitals

- One unreported fall

- A med pass she'd been pressured to backdate

- All from a shift that ended with a patient coded and resuscitated—but barely

She wasn't the one who made the errors.

She was the one who watched it happen.

And now, she had a choice.

The hallway was quiet.

Late afternoon. End-of-shift fatigue in the walls.

Voices buzzed from behind the door—admin laughing at something. Not about patients.

Never about patients.

Kayla reached for the handle.

Paused.

Imagined what would happen next:

- A thank-you for speaking up?

- A real investigation?

- Or a vague HR statement and her next six schedules cut to skeletons?

She tightened her grip on the folder.

Then let it go.

Tucked it into her bag.

And walked away.

That night, she found Callie outside the med room. Alone. Charting with one hand, chewing on a pen cap like it was keeping her from screaming.

Kayla hesitated. Then said:

"I almost turned something in today."

Callie didn't look up. "Why didn't you?"

Kayla swallowed.

"Because I knew exactly what they'd do to me."

Pause.

"And because I didn't know if you'd still stand next to me if I didn't."

Callie finally looked at her.

Eyes clear.

Voice level.

"You don't need to be a whistleblower to be in the fight."
"Then what do I need to be?"
"Awake."

Kayla nodded once.

Not like someone convinced.

Like someone called forward.

Chapter Nineteen: Shift Change

It started with donuts.

Boxed. Branded. Still warm.

Someone from admin wheeled them into the breakroom mid-morning like peace offerings. "Just a small thank you," the note read, signed by no one.

Callie stared at the pink frosting like it was a dare.

"Oh good," Rhonda muttered, "a morale pacifier. Tastes like suppressed lawsuits and diabetes."

Tasha whispered, "They brought fruit last week. Are we being courted or euthanized?"

Jules held up her phone, scrolling. "Town hall's posted for Friday. New location, new title. Ready for it?"

Callie raised an eyebrow. "Hit me."

"*Partners in Wellness: The Future of Collaborative Care Culture.*"

Callie choked on a sip of coffee. "Who's writing these, AI trained on gaslighting manuals?"

The new shift nurse came in late.

Not to work. To *sit in the breakroom*—badge flipped, not assigned.

She was older. Calm. Had the air of someone who'd watched administrations rise and fall, and never stopped charting pain meds.

"Name's Teresa," she said, nodding to Callie. "I'm retired now. But back in the day, I did twenty years here. ICU, preceptor, incident review."

Jules leaned against the wall. "What brings you back?"

Teresa held up her phone, screen glowing with the article. The one. Raine's.

"I saw this. I cried. And then I drove here."

Callie blinked. "Seriously?"

Teresa nodded. "You're not crazy. You're not wrong. You're just saying what we couldn't."

Then she reached into her tote and pulled out a manila folder.

"I kept copies," she said. "Of incident reports that never went past Risk. Years ago. Before you even started."

The room went silent.

"Names redacted. But the pattern's there."

Melissa took the folder.

Jules scanned the first few pages and exhaled like she'd been holding her breath for ten years.

"This is…" she whispered, "proof."

Teresa nodded. "Call it what it is. A handoff."

The QR board broke a record that week—over 10,000 entries.

Callie's name had gone viral again, this time in a TikTok video stitched together with screenshots, audio from the article, and a soundtrack that somehow made anger feel like worship.

Her face wasn't in it.

But her words were.

> *"We're not burned out. We're being burned alive."*

Kayla messaged her. Just one line:

"I was wrong. But I'm here now. If there's still space."

Callie replied:

"Always."

Friday came.

The town hall was packed.

A PowerPoint flickered on the screen—shades of blue, corporate fonts, the same vocabulary of "resilience" and "gratitude" they'd heard since before Dorothy died.

Someone in the front row raised their hand.

It was Tasha.

Voice clear. Hands still.

> "Why are we just now talking about wellness when we've been screaming into the void for years?"

The admin rep froze. Smiled too wide.

"Well, as you know, we're evolving as an organization."

> "No," Tasha said, louder now. "You're scrambling."

Someone clapped.

Then another.

Then Rhonda stood and said, "You wanna show support? Start with safe ratios. Not pastries."

Callie didn't speak.

She didn't need to.

She just stood, met the eyes of the woman on stage, and nodded once.

> *You see us now.*

And the woman?

She looked away.

That night, Callie got a text from Raine.

> *Next article's already in draft. Working title:*
> *"Shift Change: What Happens When*
> *Nurses Refuse to Be Quiet."*
> *Want a preview?"*

Callie typed back:

> *No. I want to keep going.*

Chapter Twenty: The Walls Speak

The message came through the board.

No signature. No sender ID. Just the subject line:

I work in the building. I see everything.

Callie almost dismissed it—another anonymous post, probably just someone blowing off steam. But the body of the message stopped her cold.

> *I've seen the incident reports disappear.*
> *I've been in the meetings where they strategize how to "soften the blow."*
> *I'm not a nurse. I'm not a doctor. I'm admin.*
> *And I'm done pretending this is okay.*

Attached: a PDF.

Redacted notes from internal calls.

Rephrased directives from Risk and PR.

> *"Frame it as miscommunication. Don't use the word understaffed. Ever."*

> *"We can't be seen retaliating—but realign her schedule."*

> *"Shift focus to staff appreciation. Build a buffer against bad press."*

Jules read it over her shoulder and let out a low whistle.

"Well," she said, "looks like the walls don't just have ears—they've grown a conscience."

Melissa looped in Raine by that afternoon.

The article's follow-up was already simmering. This? This was kindling.

Raine replied with one line:

> *"Confirmed. Cross-referencing language with two previous whistleblower documents from unrelated hospitals. Same tone. Same patterns. This is systemic."*

Inside the hospital, the atmosphere went from tight to twitchy.

Leadership canceled the next department-wide huddle "due to scheduling conflicts."

Emails suddenly emphasized **grateful language**. Breakroom posters updated overnight: new fonts, new smiles, new slogans.

"We Hear You. We See You. Let's Build Together."

"Let's build together," Rhonda muttered, reading one. "Who wrote this, a cult recruiter with Canva Pro?"

Callie didn't laugh.

Because this time, the silence around her wasn't passive.

It was watching.

She could feel it—like walking into a patient room and knowing, instinctively, something's about to crash.

The difference was this time *she* was the code.

She found Kayla in the elevator lobby, staring out the window at the staff parking lot.

"They're trying to flip the narrative again," Callie said.

Kayla didn't argue.

"They offered me full-time again," she said instead. "Higher rate. New title. No bedside."

Callie waited.

"I said no."

That earned a long pause. Then:

"Did you say why?"

Kayla turned to face her.

"Because I'd rather fight beside the people bleeding than sit in the tower and pretend I don't hear the screams."

That night, the Echo Room was full before Callie even got there.

People standing.

People bringing friends.

People who weren't just nurses anymore—security guards, cafeteria workers, lab techs.

Everyone had a story. Now they were realizing they had each other.

Melissa stood up and said, "We got our first leak from inside."

Gasps.

And then murmurs—sharp, electric.

Jules pulled up the PDF on the projector.

Lines highlighted. Patterns circled.

Callie stood near the back, watching her fire grow faces.

Watching something bigger than her take shape.

And then someone asked:

"Do we strike?"

The room went silent.

Callie didn't answer.

Not yet.

But she didn't walk away, either.

Chapter 20.5 – Snap Line

It was after a rebuild session.

Whiteout had been hit again.

Posts pulled. Server slowed. Traffic throttled.

And Callie was ready to throw her laptop across Melissa's garage.

But Jules?

Jules just… sat.

Still. Too still.

The others had left.

Only Callie remained, half-heartedly scrolling code fragments and sipping cold coffee.

That's when Jules spoke.

> "Do you know I once reported a surgeon for operating after a dose of Ativan?"

Callie looked up, caught off guard.

Jules didn't wait for permission to continue.

"Patient died.
Chart said 'expected complication.'

My report? Never made it past the first round.
I found it in the shred bin two weeks later—torn, but still legible."

She didn't cry.

Didn't blink fast.

She just breathed like each inhale cost her something.

"I thought maybe if I stuck around long enough, played the game, I'd change it from the inside. Be the quiet reformer."

Callie didn't speak.

Jules turned to her.

"Then you showed up. Loud. Raw. Furious.

And I realized—I'd become the kind of nurse who tells others to be careful instead of brave."

Callie stepped closer.

"You didn't fail."

Jules laughed. Bitter. Not cruel.

"Didn't I?"

She picked up a pen, started absentmindedly clicking it.

"You're the leader I wasn't.
The one who didn't wait for permission."

Pause.

"I'm proud of you, Callie. But I'm also sorry.

Because watching you do this...

It reminds me what I never did."

Callie placed a hand on her shoulder.

"You're still here. That counts."
"You think it's enough?"

Callie didn't answer.

Because some questions don't have clean endings.

Chapter Twenty-One: The Burn Protocol

By now, Callie could spot the surveillance.

The subtle change in her schedule.
 The way her emails started "accidentally" bouncing.
 The way leadership reps made a habit of standing just a little too long at the nurse's station with coffee and fake smiles.

She kept notes.
 Times. Names. Words.

She was done pretending it wasn't happening.

They weren't playing chess anymore.

This was a slow burn.

And Callie had gasoline.

The latest post on the board wasn't a story.

It was a blueprint.

> *"There's no policy against a coordinated sick day."*

"No one can stop you from declining to pick up extra."

"It only takes ten of us calling out to break their flex plan."

At the bottom: a date.

Not signed.

But the room knew.

This wasn't a suggestion.

It was a burn protocol.

Melissa stood at the front of the Echo Room, whiteboard marker in hand.

"We don't use the word 'strike,'" she said. "We use 'decline.' 'Unavailable.' 'Not safe to work.'"

Tasha raised a hand. "What happens if they lock us out after?"

Jules answered without flinching. "Then we don't go back."

Silence.

Thick. Full of blood and breath and memory.

Callie looked around the room—at the techs, the nurses, even a few float pool folks who'd come on their day off.

And then she said:

> "You want safe staffing? Make them feel
> unsafe without us."

That night, the hospital posted another staff video.

Smiling faces. Piano music. Words like *"resilience"* and *"team."*

Callie watched it once. Then watched it again with the volume off and fury on full blast.

They were trying to drown the fire in stock footage and cafeteria vouchers.

But the comments told another story.

> *"I saw my sister sobbing in a supply closet
> last month. Where's that on the reel?"*

> *"No amount of B-roll fixes what they did to
> Dorothy."*

> *"Keep the video. We'll keep the receipts."*

The QR code was printed onto protest posters now.

Jules had tracked at least thirty-three facilities where stories were being uploaded by the hour.

The flood couldn't be stopped.

So the hospital tried to pretend it wasn't happening.

The plan was set.

One week.

That's all they needed.

One week of coordinated *no's.*

> No picking up.
> No last-minute stays.
> No guilt-bargaining for coverage.

They weren't calling out.

They were opting out.

Melissa said it best:

> "We've been giving blood. Now we give silence."

Two days before it launched, Callie was pulled into another meeting.

HR. Risk. Someone from PR this time, fake friendly with pearl earrings and a notepad she never actually wrote in.

"We want to support our nurses," she said. "We're concerned about some of the online rhetoric. It's dangerous. Divisive."

Callie smiled slowly.

"Dangerous?" she asked. "You mean like unreported ratios? Like flexing new grads into trauma bays?"

She leaned forward.

"You're not worried about the rhetoric. You're worried people are listening."

They didn't fire her.

But the door didn't close softly when she left.

Back in the breakroom, someone had taped a new message to the wall.

Bold black Sharpie, all caps:

**IF THEY DON'T WANT TO HEAR US,
WE'LL SHOW THEM WHAT SILENCE
REALLY FEELS LIKE.**

Callie stared at it.

Then added, below:

Seven days. No apologies.

Chapter Twenty-Two: Code Burn

It started at 06:42.

Two no-shows in telemetry. One in PACU. Three from float pool.

By 07:15, the charge nurse in Med-Surg was on the phone with staffing, her voice pinched.

> "They didn't even call out. They just… didn't pick up."

By 07:30, the internal message board was lighting up.

> *"Anyone able to pick up?"*
> *"Urgent: ICU short four nurses."*
> *"Please. Anything. Just one shift."*

By 08:00, it was clear.

No one was coming.

Callie sat in her car just outside the hospital parking structure. Coffee in one hand. Badge untouched in the other.

She didn't clock in.

She didn't have to.

This wasn't an accident.

This was a **Code Burn**.

Inside, chaos simmered.

Leadership called it an "unanticipated operational disruption." In nurse terms, it was a collapse in real time.

Manager phones blew up. The float pool thread was dead silent.

The QR board? **Exploding**.

> *"They begged for our labor, not our lives."*
> *"One day. One voice. Ten thousand choices to say NO."*
> *"This is what you built. Now survive it without us."*

No names. No leaders.

But Callie could feel it in her blood:

This wasn't a walkout.

This was a *shutoff valve*.

And leadership had just learned what it felt like to bleed.

Rhonda texted first.

RHONDA:
*ER has four nurses for 36 patients. They
called a Code White.
Admin's pretending it's a power outage. It's
not. It's us.*

CALLIE:
*Tell them we're still alive. Just done dying
quietly.*

At 10:07 a.m., the hospital released a statement to
internal staff:

*"We acknowledge the strain today's
unavailability has placed on operations. We
are initiating emergency protocol to ensure
safe patient care. Your continued
commitment is deeply appreciated."*

Callie laughed—sharp, humorless.

"You don't appreciate us," she muttered to the
windshield. "You just miss the cover we gave you."

Melissa held the Echo Room live online that day.

Screens lit up with nurses from five different states.

Someone called in from a supply closet in Oregon.

Another whispered from their car in Florida.

Jules ran the chat, sorting intel. Tasha tracked who was still being threatened. Raine was already building the next article.

Callie didn't speak until the end.

And when she did?

> "Let them call it chaos," she said. "But we know it's clarity.
>
> We know what it feels like now—to be missing on purpose.
>
> And we're not done."

By that evening, hospitals in thirteen different cities had reported "unusual staffing shortages."

And by morning, new QR codes were up—on city buses, light posts, bathroom stalls.

Someone made stickers.

Someone else made shirts.

"I'm Not Burned Out. I'm Burned."

Callie didn't wear one.

She didn't need to.

Because when she walked into the grocery store later that night, two separate people looked at her and said,

"Thank you."

And she realized something dangerous:

They recognized her.

Not just her face.

Her *fight.*

Chapter 22.5 – The Day I Shut Up

The hallway was too quiet.

Shift change usually brought the noise—heels clacking, phones ringing, that one nurse who always sang "Living on a Prayer" off-key during chart checks.

But not today.

Today felt… held.

Like the air knew something.

Rhonda leaned against the wall near the elevators, arms crossed, mouth shut.

That alone was strange enough.

Callie caught her eye.

"You alright?"

Rhonda shrugged.

"Define alright."

Her tone was flat. Not funny.

Callie stepped closer. "I've seen you crack jokes during GI bleeds and elevator fires. You don't go quiet."

Rhonda looked down at her shoes—cheap black clogs with a rip near the arch.

"I shut up once.
For good reason, I thought."

"A new grad made a med error.
No harm, thank God. But admin was circling like sharks.

I covered for her.
Said I double-checked it. Took the hit."

Pause.

"I thought I was helping.

They fired her anyway.
Said I wasn't 'reliable.'

She left nursing. I stayed. Told myself she couldn't handle it."

She looked up at Callie.

"But the truth?

That day, I shut up to keep my job.
And I never really started talking again."

Callie didn't fill the space.

Didn't deflect.

She let the silence sit with them—not as punishment, but as proof that not every confession needs commentary.

Rhonda finally sighed.

> "The jokes? CPR for my soul, babe.
> Don't mistake them for peace."

The elevator dinged.

Neither of them moved.

Not yet.

Because the world could wait a few more seconds for a woman learning to speak again.

Chapter Twenty-Three: Blackout Rounds

The board went dark at 3:12 a.m.

No warning.

No glitch.

Just gone.

The QR code stopped redirecting.
 Every backup link crashed.
 Every mirror site redirected to a blank page with a single message:

> *"This site has been removed for violating terms of service."*

No one said it out loud.

But everyone knew.

Someone reported it.

And not just anyone—someone *inside*.

Callie woke to 47 text messages and a screen full of chaos.

"Is it just me?"
"Where's the backup?"
"They pulled it. Those bastards actually pulled it."

By the time she hit the Echo Room server, Jules and Tasha were already live-tracking IP logs.

Rhonda was swearing in three languages.

Melissa just sat there. Staring at her screen. Silent.

"They didn't just pull the board," she said. "They're trying to erase the proof."

An hour later, Raine confirmed it.

"Coordinated takedown request. Filed as 'internal sabotage of patient confidence and organizational integrity.' Someone gave them a backdoor."

"We're dealing with someone who knows our infrastructure. Admin didn't guess this. They knew where to hit."

Someone flipped.

Someone who once stood in the room with them.

Leadership held a "wellness check-in" at 11 a.m.

Callie didn't go.

But she heard what happened.

Staff were told the QR board had been compromised.
That it was "no longer safe."
That *any participation moving forward would be treated as insubordination.*

They didn't threaten lawsuits.

They didn't need to.

Everyone felt it in their skin.

That afternoon, Kayla found Callie in the back stairwell, a place now sacred for breakdowns and truths.

"They're blaming me."

Callie froze. "What?"

"They said because I still talk to you, I must've leaked something."

Callie shook her head. "You didn't."

"I know that. You know that. But they don't care."

Kayla looked up, eyes bloodshot. "They're trying to isolate you. Make you the problem. Then cut you off from everyone else."

Callie let the silence hang.

Then said, "Let them."

The next version of the board went live twelve hours later.

Jules built it.

Encrypted. Peer-to-peer. Untraceable.

> "If they want to shut us down, they're gonna have to rip out the entire internet."

Rhonda stood over her shoulder, grinning. "Can we make the background black this time? I want it to look like a digital funeral."

Callie nodded.

> "Not a funeral.
>
> A resurrection."

They called the new board The Anonymous Board.

When they try to blackout the truth, we bring the truth.
We erase their lies. We write in red.

Submissions came in instantly.

Faster than before.

Fiercer.

This wasn't quiet grief anymore.

It was revenge.

Callie didn't cry when the first board was taken down.

She didn't scream when she saw the silence spreading like a virus.

She just started over.

And when the first new entry hit the screen—

"They deleted our voices. But not our memories."

She whispered back:

"Let's give them something they can't erase."

Chapter Twenty-Four: The Shield

It was supposed to be a normal shift.

Tasha was covering Med-Surg. Just twenty minutes into report when she got called to the manager's office.

She didn't come back.

By the time the message reached Callie, Jules was already in motion.

> "She's in there alone," she said. "No rep. No union presence. No warning."

Callie froze. "What did they accuse her of?"

Melissa answered without looking up. "They're saying she contributed to Whiteout."

Callie blinked. "Everyone contributes to The Anonymous Board."

Jules met her eyes. "But not everyone leaves fingerprints."

They pulled her into the room an hour later.

Tasha sat in a hard plastic chair, arms crossed, face pale but dry. Across from her: two leaders Callie barely recognized and one HR rep she didn't trust even when she *was* playing nice.

"We've traced anonymous IPs tied to hospital Wi-Fi," the lead suit said. "This is a very serious breach."

Callie didn't wait for the rest.

She stepped between them.

"No," she said. "It wasn't her. It was me."

The room froze.

"I created The Anonymous Board."

It wasn't true.

Not technically.

Jules built the framework. Raine helped secure hosting. Melissa coordinated submission clearance.

But the spark? The fuel?

That had always been Callie.

"You're not even scheduled for this meeting," the HR rep said.

Callie smiled. "Guess you'll need to update your calendar."

The woman blinked.

"You just admitted to—"

"To what?" Callie snapped. "To making it harder for you to ignore dying patients? To refusing to disappear while the system devours another new grad whole?"

She stepped closer.

"You want someone to punish? Take me."

After, they made her sign something.

A statement. A document acknowledging her role in "digital instability." Terms like *administrative review, ongoing investigation,* and *suspension pending outcome* floated like smog across the paper.

She signed it with steady hands.

Tasha didn't speak the whole time.

But when Callie walked out, she followed.

That night, Raine called.

"You sure?"

Callie nodded, even though she knew Raine couldn't see her.

"Put my name in the next piece. My face. Everything."

Raine exhaled. "This isn't reversible."

"It was never supposed to be."

The article hit by morning.

The Shield: When One Nurse Takes the Fall to Protect the Rest
By Raine Ellis

Callie's photo was front and center.

Not polished.

Not staged.

Just her, on the sidewalk outside the hospital, jaw set, badge clipped but unreadable.

"They wanted a name. So I gave them mine."

The Anonymous board's traffic tripled that week.

Not because of the article.

Because of the message.

Callie wasn't just the spark anymore.

She was the shield.

And the system?

It would never unsee her again.

———

Chapter 24.5 – The Unsent Letter

She started the letter at 2:42 a.m.

In her car.

Rain tapping the windshield like it wanted to finish the sentence for her.

The dome light stayed off. The glow of her phone screen lit the cabin like a confession booth.

To Whom It May Concern,

Effective immediately, I am resigning from my position as a float nurse…

She stopped.

Deleted the sentence.

Rewrote it.

> *"…I can no longer safely or ethically function in a system that weaponizes silence and punishes truth."*

Better.

Worse.

True.

She paused halfway through.

Stared at the blinking cursor.

Then typed what she meant to say:

> I'm exhausted. Not the kind sleep can fix. The
> kind that lives in your bones like rot.
> I don't remember why I started anymore. Just
> that I don't recognize who I am now.
> And if I stay, I think I'll disappear.

A car drove past.

Headlights lit her face in the rearview mirror.

She didn't look like a rebel.

She looked like a mother trying not to break before the
morning bus came.

She didn't send the letter.

She didn't delete it either.

She saved it to her drafts.

Named it:

"Last Line."

Because maybe that's what this was.

Or maybe?

> She needed to break here… so she'd know
> how to rebuild from the truth, not the trauma.

Chapter Twenty-Five: Aftershock

The article had been live for two days.

Her face was everywhere.

Not viral, exactly. But viral enough to make rounding managers pause when she passed.

Viral enough that strangers emailed her things like

"Thank you for your bravery" and *"My sister died in that hospital. I see you."*

And viral enough that leadership went quiet.

Too quiet.

No suspension yet.
 No email.
 Just silence and surveillance.

The kind that makes you question every badge swipe, every bathroom break, every word spoken in hallways that echo too easily.

Callie kept her head down.

Mostly.

But the weight of being *seen*—not just in the system, but by everyone who'd ever heard the word nurse and assumed obedience—was heavier than she'd expected.

The Echo Room didn't meet in person that week.

Too risky.

Jules was on standby. Melissa was watching the backchannels. Rhonda took to calling herself "PR's worst nightmare" and started sketching protest sign ideas in her breaks between charting.

But Callie?

She went home.

And for the first time in a long time, she didn't feel like a nurse on break.

She felt like a woman who had set herself on fire in public.

And now she had to sit in the smoke.

Her son was doing homework at the kitchen table.

Same spot as always.

Same forehead-creased frustration over math that didn't line up neatly.

Callie sat across from him, a bowl of barely-touched pasta steaming between them.

He looked up and asked, not unkindly—

"Did you get in trouble for telling the truth?"

She blinked. "What?"

"I saw your face online. I heard you on someone's phone at school. A video. You said people were dying and no one was listening."

Callie felt her throat tighten.

She didn't deny it.

Didn't deflect.

She just stared at him.

Small. Bright. Listening.

And she realized: *this* was the risk.

Not HR.

Not admin.

Him.

What it would mean for him to grow up knowing the world had teeth.

What it would cost him to know his mom got bit for saying so.

She reached across the table.

Took his hand.

Said, "Yeah, baby. I might be in trouble."

He frowned. "Are you scared?"

She didn't lie.

"Sometimes. But not enough to shut up."

He nodded slowly. "Good."

And went back to his math.

Later that night, in the dim bathroom light, Callie looked at herself in the mirror.

No filter.
No caption.
No headline.

Just a face that had been plastered across a cause.

And the voice in her head whispered what she hadn't let herself say out loud:

> *What if it's not enough?*

What if she burned it all down and they still rebuilt it with the same rotting bricks?

What if she lost her job, her name, her safety—and it changed nothing?

What if the system could erase even this?

She didn't have answers.

But she had one truth.

> *If the system couldn't kill her fire in silence,*
> *it sure as hell couldn't do it in daylight.*

So she rinsed her face.

Tied her hair back.

And got ready for another shift.

Because the aftershock?

It only meant the ground had *moved.*

And Callie?

She was still standing on it.

Chapter 25.5 – Before the Scrubs

She wasn't a nurse yet.

Not officially.

She was 22.

Pregnant.

Terrified.

And gripping the side rail of the hospital bed like it might keep her from floating away.

The birth wasn't textbook.

It wasn't serene.

It was three shifts deep into understaffing, two hours delayed for epidural, and one nurse away from being a disaster.

Callie remembered the moment her body started to seize—not from labor.

From panic.

The OB had left.

The tech hadn't charted vitals in over an hour.

The monitor beeped too slow, and no one was answering the call light.

She wasn't scared of pain.

She was scared of being forgotten.

And then—

A nurse.

Mid-thirties.

Messy bun.

Eyes like she'd seen war and decided she wasn't dying in it.

She didn't apologize.

Didn't coo or perform comfort.

She just walked in, looked at the monitor, and said:

"You're not okay. I'm fixing that."

The nurse took over.

She paged the doctor again—aggressively.

Started a second line.

Raised Callie's legs, adjusted the fetal leads, and barked at the desk to reroute another patient.

And for the first time in hours, Callie felt seen.

Felt like she mattered.

After delivery—bloody, loud, miraculous—Callie whispered to the nurse:

> "I don't know how you do this."

The woman just smiled.

Tired. Soft. Unapologetic.

> "You will."

Callie didn't know what she meant then.

But standing years later in a hallway full of nurses refusing to disappear?

She remembered.

And she did.

Chapter Twenty-Six: The Nurse Line

It wasn't organized.

Not exactly.

No official emails. No flyers. No hashtags.

Just a shift. A silence. And a hallway.

The message had gone out the night before—one sentence, no signature:

> **"If they ask us to stand alone, let's show them what together looks like."**

They didn't march.

They showed up.

Uniforms on. Badges clipped. Eyes forward.

At 7:00 a.m., nurses from every floor stepped into the main corridor between Med-Surg and ICU and lined the walls.

No one spoke.

No chants. No shouting.

Just presence.

Like a pulse with no sedation.

Callie stood at the center, near the nurses' station where she once whispered complaints under her breath. Now she didn't whisper.

She didn't speak at all.

She let the stillness do the talking.

It was louder.

By 7:06, unit managers were peeking around corners like they'd wandered into the wrong hospital.

By 7:10, someone from HR walked past and did a double take so dramatic it could've qualified as a workplace injury.

At 7:12, someone from administration started filming. Quietly. From their phone.

Callie made eye contact with them and smiled.

That kind of smile you give when you've already buried the fear and lit a candle on top.

She caught sight of Kayla near the end of the hallway.

Not at the front.

But not hiding either.

Good.

Melissa stood across from her, arms crossed, jaw set to detonate.

Jules walked in last.

Handed Callie a folded paper as she passed.

> "The Anonymous board has been mirrored again. And someone translated it into Spanish, Arabic, and Tagalog."

Callie didn't reply.

She just nodded.

A patient transport tech passed through the hallway and stopped.

"Is this a drill?" he asked.

Rhonda—three steps down—answered without breaking posture.

> "Nope. This is what a nervous system looks like when it refuses to be numb."

The kid nodded and kept pushing his stretcher.

At 7:30 sharp, the CNO appeared.

Pressed suit. Calm expression.

The kind of calm you only wear when the ground under you is cracking and you're still trying to walk across it like it's polished marble.

They didn't speak.

Just walked down the hall.

Met every nurse's eyes.

Callie held their gaze until the very end.

And when they passed?

She didn't turn to follow.

She stayed.

It didn't last long.

Fifteen minutes, tops.

Then the line dissolved—like it had never been there at all.

Except it had.

And they all knew it.

You could scrub a floor.

You couldn't unsee that line.

Later, in the locker room, Callie sat with her hands between her knees, shaking so subtly it didn't look like fear.

It looked like voltage.

Jules sat beside her.

"You good?"

Callie shook her head. "Not even close."

Pause.

"But I'm clearer than I've ever been."

On her way out, she passed a sign on the staff board.

One of those laminated "Core Values" posters HR liked to hang like air fresheners over sewage.

But someone had added something to the bottom in Sharpie.

Big. Unapologetic.

> **YOU CAN'T LEAD PEOPLE YOU REFUSE TO SEE.**

Callie didn't smile.

She didn't cry.

She just looked at it and thought:

> *You see me now, don't you?*

Anonymous board submission

Posted anonymously. Timestamp: 3:08 a.m.

"I Got Out. But I Still Dream in Bed Alarms."

I left the hospital last year.

I gave my notice on a Monday, finished my shift, turned in my badge, and walked out without crying.

That was my win.

But I still:

Chart in my sleep
Wake up reaching for vitals
Hear call lights in songs that don't have them

Flinch when someone says "short-staffed" like it's casual

They told me leaving would fix everything.

It didn't.

It just made the guilt quieter.

Sometimes I still feel like I abandoned the war while someone else was bleeding on the floor I left behind.

But then I found the Anonymous board.

And I remembered:

We were never supposed to survive that place quietly.

Chapter Twenty-Seven: What Remains

They didn't fire her.

They didn't have to.

Instead, they stripped her shifts to skeleton status.

Pulled her from critical rooms.

Reassigned her to discharge rounding and paperwork audits—the kind of tasks you give to ghosts before you erase them altogether.

Callie didn't ask for clarification.

She knew what it was.

Administrative exile.

A slow, sterile bleed.

The badge still scanned.

The schedule still pinged.

But her presence?

It was treated like a virus.

Nurses who used to joke with her in the breakroom now gave her tight smiles and full coffee cups they didn't stay to drink.

The interns still watched her like a legend.

The managers watched her like a liability.

And the patients?

Well, they still bled the same.

She passed the nurses' station mid-shift and caught the end of a whisper.

> *"I heard she's the reason the board went down in the first place..."*

Her throat didn't tighten.

Her jaw didn't clench.

She just kept walking.

Because survival had stopped being emotional.

Now it was tactical.

At home, it hit different.

She poured cereal for dinner. Again.

Dropped her keys in the fruit bowl with a thunk that felt way too loud in a kitchen that had no music anymore.

Her son asked if she was okay.

She lied, but gently.

"I'm just tired, baby."

He nodded.

Didn't press.

But before bed, he handed her a drawing:

A stick figure in scrubs, standing in front of a fire with other smaller stick figures behind her.

A speech bubble above the figure's head:

"I got you."

Callie stared at it so long her eyes burned.

The next day, Jules pulled her into an empty room with lead-lined walls and a busted suction canister that hadn't worked in two years.

"We got the subpoena notice," she said. "They're coming for the board again."

Callie didn't flinch. "The Anonymous board?"

"Everything attached to it. And Raine's piece made it worse. We're officially a 'coordinated threat to workplace stability.'"

Rhonda's voice crackled in over speaker:

> "Well we are stable. We just don't bend over when they throw 'team-building' at us like it's morphine."

Melissa cut in:

> "They're trying to pick us off one by one. We have a choice to make."

Callie raised an eyebrow. "Which is?"

Jules met her eyes.

> "Do we fight in public now—or disappear to protect the next nurse coming up behind us?"

Callie didn't answer right away.

Because the fire inside her wasn't roaring anymore.

It was low. Controlled. Hungry.

She wasn't sure what she was anymore.

Not anonymous.

Not free.

Not safe.

But still standing.

And that counted.

More than they realized.

That night, the board glitched for the first time.

Entries wouldn't post.

The archive flickered.

The code froze for six full minutes.

Then came a message:

"You are being monitored."

Not signed.

Not traced.

Just real enough to make the silence loud again.

Callie closed her laptop.

Stared at her hands.

And whispered, to no one:

> *"You can take the tools.*
> *You can take the walls.*
> *But I remember what this feels like now."*

She stood up.

> *"And I'm not the only one."*

Chapter Twenty-Eight: Signal Fire

The board was still glitching.

Posts went up, then vanished.

Archives froze.

Someone had uploaded a black square with white text that just read:

"If our silence is a threat, then hear us now."

That one stayed up.

Even when everything else flickered out.

Callie stood outside the hospital, watching the sunrise smear blood orange across the sky.

Her badge was still in her pocket.

But she hadn't swiped in.

Not yet.

Not today.

Inside, they'd started a new "culture survey."

Color-coded feedback boxes. Anonymous comment sections with reminders like "Please keep responses constructive."

One nurse wrote:

"We are out of blood to be constructive with."

It got deleted within the hour.

Jules met her in the parking structure, leaning against her car like a secret.

"They're getting sloppy," she said.

Callie raised an eyebrow. "You say that like it's new."

"No—I mean really sloppy. The IT trail? We traced it. They've been flagging our accounts. Pulling messages before they're even posted."

Callie nodded once.

Not surprised.

Just… done.

"What if we stop posting?" she asked.

Jules blinked. "You wanna stop?"

"No," Callie said. "I want to broadcast."

That night, she recorded a message.

No hospital logos. No name tags. Just her, backlit by the glow of a busted desk lamp, voice steady but sharp enough to cut glass.

She didn't rehearse.

She didn't edit.

She just spoke.

> *"They told us to be quiet.*
> *They told us to be professional.*
> *They told us to speak through the right channels—*
>
> *But the right channels are clogged with the corpses of nurses who died waiting to be heard."*

She paused.

Let the silence ache.

> *"So here's my voice.*
> *Here's my face.*

And if you're listening?
Light your own fire.
Let them see the smoke."

The video went live at 7:38 p.m.

Jules uploaded it.

Rhonda added subtitles. In five languages.

Melissa mirrored it on four backup servers.

Raine embedded it in an op-ed already waiting for press approval.

> The title?
> *"The Signal Fire: When Nurses Refuse to Vanish."*

By morning, it had 112,000 views.

By noon, Callie's face was on a protest poster in another state.

By dinnertime, she had a voicemail from a hospital in Chicago:

> *"We saw you. We're next."*

She sat on the floor of her bedroom that night, the weight finally catching up.

Not breaking her.

Just pressing in—like gravity that now had her name on it.

Her son peeked in.

Held up his tablet.

"Mom… is this you?"

She nodded.

"Are you in trouble?"

Pause.

"Maybe. But not the kind that stops things. The kind that starts them."

He came over. Sat down next to her.

No more questions.

Just quiet.

Thick. Holy. Honest.

The kind of quiet that meant everything had changed.

Chapter Twenty-Nine: Wildfire

It didn't start with a post.

It started with a middle finger and a Sharpie.

Someone taped a sheet to the breakroom fridge:

> "I'm not covering for your short-staffing anymore.
> This is not a favor. This is a funeral."

No signature.

No preamble.

But it lit the room like gasoline.

By noon, someone in OB refused to flex.

Then two in ED.

Then half the float pool called in "emotionally unfit for safe care delivery."

They didn't use the word strike.

But the hospital did.

And that's when things caught fire.

Callie walked onto her unit and didn't speak.

She didn't have to.

The charge nurse handed her the assignment sheet with two rooms circled in red.

"You've been pulled again. Management wants you on observational rounding."

Callie smiled.

The kind of smile that belongs to someone who's about to make a problem out of being ignored.

"Sure. I'll round. On every patient I'm not assigned because this place can't keep its staff."

She took the paper.

Tore it in half.

Handed it back.

"There. Consider yourself rounded."

Someone clapped.

She didn't look to see who.

Didn't need applause.

She needed traction.

Whiteout was a wildfire now.

Raine's article was picked up by a news affiliate in Detroit.

A traveling nurse from San Diego created a "Burned Not Broken" TikTok montage that hit 2.1 million views in under a day.

The soundtrack?

Callie's voice from the Signal Fire video, over slow motion footage of nurses walking out of hospital doors.

Not angrily.

Purposefully.

Rhonda sent a text to the Echo Room group chat that just read:

"Too late to apologize now, isn't it?"

At 3:14 p.m., security was called to the second floor.

Not for violence.

Not for theft.

For a line of nurses standing silently with signs.

Not protesting.

Presenting.

Each one held a printout of a patient story from the original QR board—names redacted, details blurred, but every single one real.

Callie stood in the center.

Hers read:

> "I charted death in four-hour increments and got a pizza party."

Leadership showed up with walkie-talkies and forced smiles.

They said things like "Let's talk this out" and "We're on your side."

Callie didn't answer.

She held the sign higher.

Because at this point?

Talking was a trap.

Visibility was the weapon.

The next day, hospitals in five other states staged flash "truth lines."

No union.

No plan.

Just nurses standing still.

Holding up the stories that the administration tried to delete.

That night, Callie walked through her front door and didn't fall apart.

She microwaved leftover spaghetti.

Watched her son play Roblox with the sound off.

Checked Whiteout.

Checked Raine's messages.

Read another thousand submissions that said the same thing, in different handwriting:

"We thought we were alone.
Then we saw her."

Callie set her phone down.

Took a deep breath.

And laughed.

Not because it was funny.

Because it was real.

Because for the first time in years, they weren't backing down.

And neither was she.

Chapter Thirty: Exposure

The press release dropped at 8:01 a.m.

> "We are aware of ongoing social media commentary surrounding nurse culture. While we respect the voices of our clinical staff, recent behaviors do not reflect the values of our institution. Our commitment to integrity remains unchanged."

It was a masterclass in deflection.

Nothing said.

Everything implied.

Callie read it over stale breakroom coffee while someone down the hall cried behind a closed supply room door.

She didn't react.

Just folded the memo into thirds and slid it under the sharps container where it belonged.

By 10:00 a.m., Whiteout was glitching again.

Not by accident.

Jules pinged her from two floors up:

JULES:
Someone tried to override admin controls. It's internal.
They're not just watching now. They're inside.

Callie didn't flinch.

She messaged Raine instead:

"They're coming hard."

RAINE:
"So do we.
I'm almost done with the leak package.
Are you ready to publish hell?"

It hit at 3:15 p.m.

Headlined on every major board:

"THE COST OF SILENCE: INTERNAL
DOCUMENTS FROM A SYSTEM THAT KNEW
BETTER."

Raine didn't hold back.

Emails showing management scrubbing incident reports.

Meeting minutes that casually mentioned "protecting donor optics."

A scanned memo advising managers not to "escalate nurse concerns unless media interest is confirmed."

There was even a death listed in Risk Review: a patient with a med error flagged—then unflagged—after a "donor contact request."

The hashtags exploded.

#NotJustBurnout

#DyingOnTheClock

#WhiteoutWasRight

Callie didn't read the comments.

She couldn't.

Not right now.

Because home was loud tonight.

Her middle son had a science project that involved baking soda and a bottle that somehow exploded sideways onto the ceiling.

The youngest was crying because someone stole his in-game armor again.

The oldest kept asking her if she'd seen the new video of herself, someone remixed with protest chants.

She hadn't.

She was still wiping vinegar off the kitchen tile.

"You okay, Mom?" the middle one asked.

She almost said yes.

Then stopped.

"No," she said. "But I'm still showing up."

At midnight, she sat in her car outside the hospital.

Alone.

Lights off.

She scrolled through Raine's article again—slow, surgical.

Paused on the last paragraph:

"What we normalize becomes policy.
What we bury becomes practice.
What we survive becomes precedent.

They knew. They chose.
And now we choose to expose."

Callie leaned back.

Closed her eyes.

And whispered:

"Let them see what they built."

Because exposure wasn't the end.

It was the match.

Chapter Thirty-One: The Leak

They didn't see it coming.

They thought the leak was the article.

But it wasn't.

The article was a spark.

This was combustion.

At 8:47 a.m., an anonymous email hit every inbox in the hospital's internal staff directory.

Subject line:

> "You Deserve to Know What's Been Hidden."

The attachment?

A 67-page internal audit labeled **CONFIDENTIAL.**

Contents:

- Retaliation reports buried in "staff behavior" files

- Patient complaints labeled "resolved" with no evidence of follow-up

- A physician flagged for repeated safety violations—still active, still protected

One page showed direct language:

"Do not elevate concern to the media without administrative filter."

"Pre-clear all nurse-facing memos with legal."

"Discredit internal disruptors before escalation."

The hospital denied everything.

Issued a statement by noon:

"An unauthorized document has been circulated containing outdated or unverified information. We urge staff to refrain from speculation and to focus on patient care."

Translation:

Shut up. Show up. Pretend you didn't see it.

Callie saw it.

Callie printed it.

Three copies.

One for Jules.

One for Melissa.

One taped inside her locker like armor.

By mid-shift, admin started pulling people into one-on-ones again.

Tasha. Rhonda. Even that soft-spoken night nurse from PACU who hadn't spoken up in months.

They weren't subtle.

They were making a list.

And Callie?

She wasn't on it.

Yet.

Back in the stairwell, she met Jules.

"There's more," Jules said. "Someone else came forward. Teresa."

Callie blinked. "The retired nurse?"

"She's got receipts. Old-school ones. Paper trails. Incident reports from her last five years—stuff that never made it to digital."

Callie's stomach turned.

Not from fear.

From rage.

Because they'd buried this so deep, they thought time would eat the truth.

But Teresa?

She archived it.

Like evidence. Like a future war.

That night, Raine went live with Part II of her exposé.

Title:

> **"The Ledger: What They Buried While Nurses Bled."**

Callie didn't even have time to read the full piece before her phone started vibrating off the table.

By the end of the hour:

A state rep had tweeted it.

A nurse from another city DM'd her:
"We just found the same thing."

Her ex sent a single text:
"So this is what you've been doing? Jesus, Callie."

She left it on read.

At home, the boys were loud.

Normal.

Bickering over screen time and snacks.

But the youngest—her wild one—came up behind her, holding her phone.

"You're famous," he said.

Callie raised an eyebrow. "Is that good?"

He shrugged.

"You're mad on TV. I think that's cool."

She laughed. Just once.

Dark and dry and too real to fake.

She stood at the sink later, hands in soapy water, head spinning.

And thought:

I didn't ask for this.

Then:

But maybe I was built for it.

Because the leak wasn't just a story anymore.

It was a damn flood.

And if the hospital thought they could sweep this under, they were about to drown in it.

Chapter Thirty-Two: The Offer

The email subject line was clean.

"Exploratory Opportunity – Leadership Pathway Conversation"

No threats. No accusations.

Just an invitation.

To talk.

Callie read it three times before closing her phone and tossing it into the laundry basket like it might infect her clothes.

She didn't respond.

Not right away.

Because she knew what it was.

It wasn't an opportunity.

It was a muzzle.

Wrapped in flattery and framed like progress.

They met in a conference room that smelled like antiseptic and deflection.

The walls had those "inspirational" posters:

A mountain. A river. A climber with perfect hair.

The CNO sat at the end of the table, flanked by two suits and a "staff liaison" she'd never seen before.

They smiled too much.

Callie didn't.

"We want to partner with you," the CNO began.
"This isn't about control—it's about collaboration."
"You've got a voice, and we believe in amplifying that in the right direction."

Callie said nothing.

They kept going.

"What if you took a formal role? Help guide policy change? Be the face of our staff reform initiative?"

There it was.

The offer.

A title.

A salary bump.

A seat at the same table that kept telling her to be grateful for pizza parties while people died on hallway beds.

She didn't say no.

Not yet.

Because part of her—the tired part—wanted to say yes.

Wanted to believe this could be how change happens.

Wanted the insurance, the structure, the illusion of safety.

That night at home, her sons were all there.

The oldest scrolling through protest coverage online.

The middle one asked how to make spaghetti "without making it taste like soap."

The youngest crawling into her lap and whispering:

"You're not gonna stop, right?"

Callie froze.

"Stop what?"

He shrugged.

"Fighting."

She didn't answer.

He hugged her tight.

"'Cause if you do, they win."

Later, she stood in the kitchen, light off, looking out at the backyard she barely had time to notice anymore.

And whispered to the dark:

"What if I'm too tired to keep going?"

The silence answered back:

"Then let them carry you until you remember why you started."

The next morning, she sent her reply.

Simple. Clear.

"I don't want a seat at your table.

I want to flip the damn thing over."

They never wrote back.

But she felt the system tense.

Like it realized it couldn't buy her off.

Like it finally knew it couldn't stop what it didn't build.

Chapter Thirty-Three: No More Quiet

It started with a video.

Grainy. Unedited. Shot on a phone propped up against a bedside table.

A nurse in a breakroom.

Hair messy. Scrubs wrinkled.

Eyes wrecked.

> *"I watched a patient code while I was taking vitals on two others.*
> *I cried in the med room for six minutes, then kept going.*
>
> *They said that was resilience.*
>
> *It was neglect. Systemic. And sanctioned."*

She posted it with the hashtag:

#NoMoreQuiet

By noon, there were forty more.

Different faces. Different accents.

Same war.

A nurse from Boston whispered through tears, "I'm so damn tired of surviving things they pretend never happened."

A night tech in Texas showed his work shoes—cracked, bloodstained, still labeled from his third code that week.

A travel nurse said nothing.

Just held up a sign:

"You built this. We bleed in it."

Callie sat at the edge of her bed, phone glowing, heart thudding like it remembered what broke it in the first place.

Jules called, voice tight.

"This wasn't us. It's them."
"All of them."

Whiteout was on fire again.

Not crashing—surging.

The posts were public now.

People were putting their names. Their unit numbers. Their faces.

And still?

No one could stop it.

Because for every nurse who was afraid, there were two who were done apologizing.

Rhonda sent a message that made Callie cry for the first time in weeks.

> "I posted mine. With my name.
>
> If I lose this job, I'll sleep like I didn't lie today."

Melissa reposted Dorothy's story.

With full detail. With context. With Callie's voice overlaid from the Signal Fire video.

The caption?

> **"You're not burned out. You've been set on fire."**

It hit 1.2 million views in five hours.

That night, Callie walked into her hospital like she belonged there.

Like they didn't almost erase her.

She wasn't alone.

At least fifteen nurses wore black.

Not coordinated.

Not spoken.

Just chosen.

Mourning what they'd lost.

And daring the system to notice.

In the stairwell, Kayla stopped her.

Eyes red. Hands shaking. Phone in her hand.

> "I posted, too," she whispered. "I didn't tag you. But I told the story. The real one. About what they made us do. About the mom we lost. About the baby who never got a name."

Callie didn't speak.

She just reached out and pulled her into the kind of hug that hurt—because it held every silence they'd ever swallowed.

That night, after the kids were asleep, Callie sat at her desk and opened her inbox.

Hundreds of messages.

Nurses.

Techs.

Moms.

Sons.

One read:

> *"My daughter was one of them.*
> *The kind who died before anyone listened.*
>
> *I saw your face.*
>
> *Now I'm not quiet either."*

Callie's breath caught.

And for the first time, she didn't feel like she was burning alive.

She felt like a fire line.

Holding back the dark.

Chapter Thirty-Four: The Breaking Point

The first sign was the email.

No header. No greeting. Just:

> "Your license has been flagged for review by the state board. You will be contacted shortly."

No reason.

No detail.

Just enough threat to make her stomach drop.

The second sign was worse.

Her youngest's school called mid-shift.

> "There was an anonymous report made to child protective services.
>
> They're saying there may be neglect."

Callie didn't respond.

Because rage and shock are siblings.

And both of them had her by the throat.

She left work without clocking out.

Didn't even tell the charge nurse.

By the time she got home, there was a card on the door.

Plain. White. CPS stamped on the front like a bruise.

She sat in the hallway while her kids played Minecraft in the next room.

Melissa texted first.

MELISSA:
"They're coming for your foundation now. Not just your job. Your life."

Jules followed:

JULES:
"This is war. And you're the headline they want to erase."

Callie didn't respond.

Because there were no words for what it feels like to be punished for telling the truth in a way that puts your children in the crossfire.

Later, she stood in the kitchen with one hand on the counter and the other clutching a CPS form that said absolutely nothing but felt like everything.

And whispered:

"You said I was dangerous. You had no idea."

She didn't sleep that night.

She built.

With Jules.

With Raine.

With Teresa, who dropped three more damning memos on a shared drive like they were grenades.

They uploaded everything.

Not just stories.

Scans. Photos. Emails. Logs.

Callie added one more thing:

A video.

It wasn't angry.

It was lethal.

> *"You came for my kids.*
> *You came for my license.*
> *You came for my life.*
>
> *You should have just come for my badge.*
> *Because I can live without that.*
> *I can't live quiet."*

She posted it.

Didn't check the numbers.

Didn't check the comments.

Just packed a go bag, dropped her sons off with her sister, and went back to work like nothing had changed.

Because everything had.

Inside the hospital, it was silent.

Not out of tension.

Out of respect.

They knew.

Everyone knew.

Even the ones who used to look away.

Rhonda handed her a note during shift report.

One line:

> "We're done watching you stand alone."

That night, the nurses stayed after hours.

All of them.

Black scrubs. Silent.

And when Callie walked in?

They clapped.

Not loud.

Just long.

Long enough to mean:

"We saw.
We're still here.
And we're not leaving."
_____

Chapter 34.5 – The Meeting They Didn't Prepare For

They invited her to the table again.

Not the first time.

Not even the second.

But this time, she accepted.

Not because she trusted them.

Because she'd already read the minutes from last week's meeting.

Same words, different lies.

> "Safety culture."
> "Staff partnership."
> "Ongoing improvement strategies."

They didn't expect her to speak.

They expected her to nod.

Callie stood before they could finish the opening slide.

Held up a copy of the leaked Risk memo with admin's name still watermarked in the corner.

"This? This is what we survived under."

She dropped it on the table like a body.

Then pulled out a second sheet.

"Here's what you're going to do if you want to keep anyone left on your payroll."

The list was short.

- Independent incident review board.

- Whistleblower protection policy with third-party enforcement.

- Safe staffing commitment clause tied to leadership bonuses.

No fluff. No compromise.

They stared at her.

She stared back.

"You can say yes now.
Or I walk. And I take all of them with me."

Silence.

Someone shifted in a chair.

Someone else cleared their throat.

The CNO looked tired. Maybe scared.

Finally:

"We'll need legal to review—"

Callie cut in.

"You've had months."

She stood.

"This is the final offer.
You say no? Whiteout goes federal."

No yelling.

No slamming doors.

Just paper and consequence.

The next day, the first item on the hospital's internal newsletter read:

> **Effective immediately, we are instituting new nurse-led safety protocols and creating an independent clinical reporting body.**

There was no mention of her name.

No picture.

Just the policy.

And that was the win.

Callie didn't celebrate.

She drove home.

Took her shoes off at the door.

And for the first time in a year, didn't check her phone before bed.

She'd already said what needed saying.

And now?

They were repeating her words.

That meant she'd already won.

_____

Chapter Thirty-Five: What We Build

They didn't shut the hospital down.

There was no dramatic overhaul. No news cameras on the lawn. No villain escorted out in cuffs.

That's not how real revolutions land.

They don't end in fireworks.

They start with fire.

And leave smoke that never quite clears.

But things did change.

Policies were rewritten.

Silenced incident reports were unburied.

An "external transparency board" was created—lipstick on liability—but Callie made damn sure real nurses sat on it.

The Anonymous board was no longer underground.

It was open-source.

Archived in four countries. Mirrored by nurse coalitions. Taught in two nursing schools as part of a "professional activism" seminar.

They'd tried to kill the story.

And instead?

It became part of the curriculum.

Callie didn't get a promotion.

She didn't want one.

But she did get a new title:

> *Advisor – Nurse Advocacy and Safe Practice Collective*

Unofficial.

Unpaid.

Unstoppable.

She still worked shifts.

Still missed lunch.

Still had moments where her hands shook behind med carts because adrenaline is hard to unlearn.

But she wasn't invisible anymore.

And that?

That changed everything.

One afternoon, she stood in the middle of the hallway—same unit, same floor—and saw something that almost made her cry.

A new grad.

Speaking up.

To her preceptor.

About a patient assignment that didn't feel safe.

And the preceptor?

Listened.

No shade. No sarcasm. Just a quiet nod and a course correction.

Callie didn't interfere.

She just walked past with a little more oxygen in her chest than she'd had all week.

At home, her sons were louder than ever.

That was a good thing.

Loud meant alive.

Loud meant free.

They didn't ask about CPS anymore.

Didn't flinch when the mail came.

Her oldest had started calling her "the rebellion lady" whenever her face showed up on someone's For You page.

She rolled her eyes every time.

But inside?

It felt like a medal.

One night, she sat outside—porch light off, wind cutting just enough to remind her she was still here—and re-read the last message she ever got from Raine before the reporter disappeared offline to work on something "big."

It read:

> "They were right. You were dangerous.
> You just chose to aim that danger at the system
> instead of letting it kill you."

She didn't respond.

Didn't need to.

Instead, she opened her laptop and checked the Whiteout dashboard.

New entries still flowing in.

Not as fast.

Not as frantic.

But steady.

Like breath.

Like resuscitation.

She clicked the newest post.

Anonymous.

Short.

One line.

"I thought I was alone. Then I saw her."

Callie didn't smile.

Didn't cry.

She just closed the screen.

Leaned back.

And whispered:

"Then keep watching.

We're not done yet."

Epilogue

Six months later.

Different city.

Different badge.

Same silence.

3M

The nurse sat in her car, watching the hospital entrance like it might lunge.

She hadn't even clocked in yet.

Already, she was drowning in the numbers.

Seven patients.

Three admits.

No tech.

One float nurse who looked like she hadn't slept since the pandemic.

She opened her phone.

Not to text.

Not to scroll.

Just to breathe.

［3M］

The Anonymous board was still live.

Quiet these days.

But not dead.

She scrolled to a random post.

January. Kansas City.

> "We stopped asking for change. We became it."

She didn't know who wrote it.

Didn't need to.

Because in that sentence—in that fire-smoke honesty—she recognized herself.

［3M］

She closed her eyes.

Took one breath.

Then another.

And walked in.

Head high.

Heart armored.

Voice—ready.

Because someone, somewhere, had lit the way.

And she wasn't going in silent.

Post-Epilogue — Raine

Three states over.

Same rot.

Raine sat in the back of a courthouse records office, surrounded by dust and bureaucracy.

She wasn't dressed like a journalist.

She never did when the stakes were real.

Today, she was just another quiet woman with a laptop and a stare that didn't blink fast enough.

The clerk had handed her the files reluctantly.

"That's all that's public," he'd said.

But Raine knew how to read between blacked-out lines.

One page caught her eye.

An incident report.

Medication error.

Fatal.

Flagged for peer review, then dismissed as "resolved."

Same phrasing.

Same formatting.

Same hospital system.

[3M]

She leaned back.

Opened a second folder.

Inside: a copy of the whistleblower memo from Callie's case—the one that cracked everything open.

Same language.

Same damage control.

Same silence.

[3M]

She opened her laptop.

Logged in.

The Anonymous board still worked.

The dashboard was quiet—but not empty.

New reports trickled in.

From nurses. From techs. From grieving families who'd found the site buried in Reddit threads and TikTok comments.

> "This isn't over," one post read.
> "It just hasn't reached your hospital yet."

3M

Raine cracked her knuckles.

Opened a fresh doc.

Titled it:

> "The Sequel: How Silence Crosses State Lines."

And typed the first line:

> "The story didn't end with Callie.
> It just changed names."

She closed the file.

Picked up her recorder.

And walked out.

Back into the system that still thought it could hide.

Printed in Dunstable, United Kingdom